P9-CEC-703

Suddenly there was the sharp, unmistakable crack of a gun, then another shot. Tony jumped to his feet.

He reached for his revolver, raced to the door with the gun in his hand. He paused in the hall, pressed against the wall while his eyes became accustomed to the interior. A door burst open opposite him as a woman somewhere in the house screamed. A man ran out of the room, pulling at his pants, his face misshapen with fright. A completely nude girl stepped to the door, slammed it. A key turned in the lock. Tony started toward the front door gripping his gun. A woman in negligee raced through the door of the parlor and ran toward the back of the house, screaming, her mouth wide open. Tony couldn't see any of the three men who'd come with him. Where the hell were those bastards?

He felt a tingling excitement running through him. He ran toward the open door of the parlor as a man leaped through it into the hallway. Tony saw the dull gleam of light from a gun in the man's hand. The guy stopped, stared at Tony.

"Romero!" he yelled. "You son of a bitch!" He yanked up his gun.

For a fraction of a second Tony hesitated. As if the motions were slowed down to half their normal speed, Tony saw the other man's gun swing up, point at him. Tony jumped to his right, slamming into the far wall as the gun in the hand of the man ten feet away blasted at him, flame spurting from the muzzle. Tony felt the light touch at the shoulder of his coat, saw the spurt of flame, heard the slug smack into the wall far behind him, and then his own gun roared in his hand...

The
PEDDLER

by **Richard S. Prather**

A HARD CASE CRIME NOVEL

A HARD CASE CRIME BOOK
(HCC-027)
December 2006

Published by

Dorchester Publishing Co., Inc.
200 Madison Avenue
New York, NY 10016

in collaboration with Winterfall LLC

*If you purchased this book without a cover, you should know
that it is stolen property. It was reported as "unsold and
destroyed" to the publisher, and neither the author nor the
publisher has received any payment for this "stripped book."*

Copyright © 1952 by Richard S. Prather
Renewed December 8, 1980 by Richard Scott Prather

Cover painting copyright © 2006 by Robert McGinnis

All rights reserved. No part of this book may be reproduced or
transmitted in any form or by any electronic or mechanical
means, including photocopying, recording or by any information storage and retrieval system, without the written
permission of the publisher, except where permitted by law.

*This book is a work of fiction. Names, characters, places, and
incidents either are the products of the author's imagination or
are used fictitiously, and any resemblance to actual events or
persons, living or dead, is entirely coincidental.*

ISBN 0-8439-5598-8
ISBN-13 978-0-8439-5598-9

The name "Hard Case Crime" and the Hard Case Crime logo
are trademarks of Winterfall LLC. Hard Case Crime books are
selected and edited by Charles Ardai.

Printed in the United States of America

Visit us on the web at www.HardCaseCrime.com

THE PEDDLER

Chapter One

Tony saw the girl as she hurried out of The Green Room on Sutter Street, turned and started walking away from him. Something about her stirred memory in his brain and he walked slowly after her, watching the black skirt swirl above her rounded calves, the slow, liquid ripple of her hips. She stopped suddenly and lit a cigarette, half turned toward him, and in the light from one of the street lamps he saw the small young face, the plump red lips and straight dark eyebrows. Now he remembered: Maria. Maria Casino.

Christ, he'd practically grown up with her here in Frisco, back on Howard Street. He grinned, remembering that first time when he was thirteen and she was fourteen, he and Joe and Whitey Kovacs had taken Maria into Kovacs' house when his folks were gone. Jesus, that was six years ago; he hadn't even seen her for almost three years. He looked her up and down from his dark, too-narrow eyes. She sure as hell hadn't been built then like she was now. He started walking toward her.

She was still standing about ten feet beyond the entrance of The Green Room, puffing on her cigarette. Tony was looking at her as he passed the entrance, so he didn't see the big guy weave out the door until the guy staggered into him. Tony jerked his head around and looked at the drunk, irritated, then turned and started to walk on. The guy grabbed Tony's arm.

"Hey," he slurred, "watch where you're goin'."

Maria turned and started to walk on down toward Powell. Tony glanced at the drunk. He was about six feet tall, heavy, with a flushed red face. His breath stank of beer and whiskey.

"Let go my arm," Tony said quietly. "You're drunk. Beat it."

The guy didn't let go. He said nastily, "Goddamn punk. Watch where yer goin'. Goin' round knocking people down. Bastard sonofabitch, watch—"

Tony, at nineteen, was five feet ten inches tall, with much of his weight in strong well-muscled arms and legs and heavy shoulders. He slammed his open right hand against the drunk's chest, bunched coat and white shirt and stringy tie in his fist, and easily yanked the bigger man close to him. He didn't say anything, but his too-narrow eyes narrowed even more and his lips pressed together in a thin, hard line. Anger jumped in his stomach; he felt like putting the slug on the bastard and rubbing his red face into the sidewalk until it was really red.

His thoughts showed in his face, in his lips and eyes and the thick bulge of muscle along his heavy jaw.

After a moment he spoke softly, savagely, to the other man. The drunk's mouth sagged open and he said, not belligerent now, "Look, forget it, fella. Let's forget it. Look, leggo."

Tony slowly uncurled his fingers, dropped his arm to his side. The drunk moved around him, keeping his eyes on Tony's face, then hurried down the sidewalk.

Tony looked down toward Powell and saw Maria walking slowly, not yet at the cross street. He hurried after her and caught up with her at the corner. He put a hand on her arm. She stopped and turned toward him, a half smile ready on her lips.

"Hi, baby," Tony said. "Where the hell you been?"

"Tony!" The half smile broadened and she put her hand over his. "Tony Romero. Where'd you come from?"

She was really sharp. Her dark brown hair was cut short and fluffed about her pale face, large brown eyes almost black against the white skin. Her lips were plump and red, and her small, even white teeth gleamed as she smiled up at him.

He said, "Just spotted you coming out of The Green Room. Damn, it's good to see you. You look like a million."

"Gee, Tony," she said, "where you been, I ain't seen you for ages."

"Knockin' around. I don't live home no more; I got outa that trap a couple years back. Never see none of the old gang no more. What you doin' now, Maria?"

She dragged on her cigarette and tossed it into the gutter. "Oh, a little of this, little of that. I ain't home no more, neither."

Tony glanced at his cheap wristwatch. It was after one in the morning. Sunday morning now. He said, "Come on, I'll buy you a drink. You got time, haven't you?"

She laughed. "I got all night, Tony."

"Good deal." He took her arm and started walking back up Sutter the way they'd come. "I got nothin' to do." He grinned. "Do it with me."

"Love to, Tony." She hung onto his arm, chattering about old times as he steered her back toward The Green Room, the nearest bar.

When they reached the entrance, she looked up and then stopped on the sidewalk. "Oh. I didn't know we were goin' here. Let's go someplace else."

"What's wrong with here? They got dark booths." He laughed.

"No...I'll tell you later. I don't like the place."

"Ah, come on, baby. One drink so I can catch up on where you been." He pulled her by the arm and she resisted at first, then went along with him, "We'll hit another spot after, if we got time," he said. She went inside with him, frowning.

The Green Room was a small place. A bar with several stools in front of it stretched along the right wall, then there was a row of booths with tables on their left, and more booths against the wall. About a dozen people, mostly men, were drinking.

After drinks had been ordered, Maria was quiet for a few seconds, then she said, "Well, what do you think, Tony?"

"About what?"

"Me being...on the hustle."

"You're a nice kid, Maria."

"Tell me the truth, Tony. You known me quite a while. Does it, well, does it make any difference to you?"

Tony squinted at her and thought about it. He considered it seriously, wondering if it did make a difference. He thought back to the times he and other kids had been with her in the empty Kovacs house and other places. And she hadn't been the only one by a long shot. So Maria was getting paid for it now, that was about the only difference.

Tony had been to the houses three or four times, but not for a couple of years. It wasn't that he saw anything wrong with it, but he didn't like paying for pretended passion; when he had a woman, he wanted her with him because she wanted it that way too.

"Well?"

"Huh? Oh, hell, I dunno, Maria, I don't see it makes no difference. You look the same's you always did— only you're about ten times prettier." Tony thought, looking at her, that she *was* damned pretty. She looked almost virginal. Her body was a woman's body, though, well-curved and soft-looking. He thought of all the men that must have kissed and caressed that body, lusted over it, slobbered on her plump lips. It didn't do anything to him—except maybe make him a little disgusted with men.

They stopped talking while the waiter served the drinks. Then she leaned forward on her elbows, smiling at him. "Tony. Tony, you're a swell guy, you know it? You're sure not gonna take nothin' from nobody, are you? You were always that way. I used to think you were great, remember? I always liked you."

He laughed. "You used to tell me you were goofy for me, baby."

"Uh huh." She looked at him for several seconds. "Maybe I never got over it."

"Yeah, you got over it, kid. Don't give me no song and dance."

They decided to go somewhere else. They finished their drinks, then walked out onto Sutter Street again. It was a cold night, the air crisp and bracing, without fog, and Maria looped her arm in Tony's as they walked to Powell and turned right toward Market Street.

Tony wondered where they'd go. He had about twenty bucks in his pocket, and no job. He'd have to work up another deal pretty soon—unless that longshot came in at Bay Meadows Monday. He had five bucks on Red Dancer to win the third. Money, he thought, the goddamn money. When was it going to happen? That question was part of Tony: When was it going to happen, when was he going to get the break?

It was something that he hung onto, waited for, the break that would get him started, put him in the big dough. It had been part of him for a long time. Tony had grown up in San Francisco pretty much as thousands of others had. He had been the "accidental" child of an Italian mother and father who rarely had enough money to feed themselves and the four other kids before Tony came, and Tony had the further common misfortune of not being wanted. He came very close to not being born at all. For a long time, as he grew up, he didn't realize that he was poor; when he did, the need for money started growing inside him. He'd quit school in the sixth grade, and in the years since then there'd been a few "deals" and a few odd jobs. Since he'd left home he'd been a laborer for a few months in a warehouse, heavy work that made him strong and also gave him and his best friend, Joe Arrigo, a chance to swipe stuff they later got rid of through a fence; he was a runner for a small bookie for a while, then he worked a few months as a bellhop in the St. Francis Hotel. He stayed there until he got too bored with it, but he had liked being around the people he thought of as having "class," the pink-skinned, well-groomed men with their fat cigars and their slim women, the slim women with sparkling wrists and fingers, and sparkling eyes. Those months at the St. Francis, naturally, only made him want money more.

The years had made him hard, tough, not only in body but in mind. He was cynical, contemptuous of the weak—perhaps because he, himself, was strong. He admired all those men who had, one way or another, amassed fortunes of money or of power. The way they got it wasn't important; the fact that they had it was. Tony's attitude toward life was woven of his belief that there were only two kinds of men: the few strong ones he thought of as at "the top," and the rest, the weak, on the bottom; and a guy had nobody but himself to blame if he stayed on the bottom. Tony had no intention of staying there.

Tony pulled a pack of cigarettes from his pocket and offered Maria one, then they stopped while he lit them both. He said, "What you want to do, Maria? Have another drink, or could you stand some chow?"

"Well, I'm a little hungry," she said.

He grinned at her. "Been workin' hard, huh?"

"Pretty hard. This is Saturday night."

"Little hungry myself. There's a place down on O'Farrell just off Market puts out the best minestrone in the world. O.K.?"

"Let's go."

She squeezed his arm and they walked the few

blocks to the Italian Restaurant. On the way they talked casually, and she told Tony she wasn't just out walking the streets; she was in one of the houses, a big place out on Fillmore.

Inside the restaurant, over huge bowls of thick, steaming minestrone, with crisp bread sticks and sliced French bread and red wine, Tony asked her, "How long you been in this racket, baby?"

"Golly, over a year now. About a year after the last time I saw you I got to going with an old guy and he finally put me up in his hotel. I just left my aunt's house—you know I was livin' with my aunt since pa married again, the crumb—and we was together about six months. I'd get these guys in a bar and take them down an alley—you know, like they were gonna get a little, they thought—and Max, that's the guy I lived with, he'd pop them one and we'd take what they had in their wallets. I never did like it, though, and finally we busted up. Well, there I was not livin' home no more, and no Max. So that's it."

"How you mean, that's it? You just start in on the hustle, just like that?"

"No, I had to see the guy runs the houses first. Got a cab driver to fix it so I could see the guy and he put me out on Church Street to start—Church Street, ain't that a laugh? I been in three, four houses before I come to the Fillmore place. In a hotel once, on call, but I make more this way."

Tony grinned. "Gettin' rich now, huh?"

"Not rich." She frowned. "They make sure we don't get rich and get out. But I made fifty tonight."

"Fifty? Fifty dollars?"

"Sure. I'da made more only I don't work only till twelve."

"Jesus," Tony said. "Fifty bucks. In just one night?" He'd never stopped to figure out how much the whores made in a night or a week. "Christ," he said, "that's *dough!*"

"I only get half, Tony. And I got lots of things to buy out of what's left. It's not bad, though." She smiled. "Better than muggin' guys in alleys."

Tony nodded somewhat absent-mindedly. Maria had started his brain working a little; he was thinking about all that dough. "What you think of the racket? You like it?"

She shrugged. "It's a job. No kicks if that's what you mean; just put in my time." She paused. "It'd be… different with you, Tony."

He laughed. "You're damn right. I wouldn't give you no dough."

"Oh, Tony! You got no idea what I'm talking about! Damn you—"

"Hey, I was havin' fun, is all." She looked and sounded angry. "Don't bust a seam."

They finished their minestrone and had some more of the red wine Tony had ordered with the meal. He sipped the wine and thought, a dozen ideas flashing through his quick brain. Then he asked Maria, "What about the rest of it—you said you only get half. Who gets the rest?"

"Guys that run the show, shift the girls around, pay off the cops. Cops get a lot of it, but that's all handled by the big guys. Fellow named Sharkey's boss of the houses, but he's under the big guys—you know, the ones that got the books and the rest of the rackets."

"Sharkey, huh?" Then Tony asked the question that was typical of Tony. "Who's the Top?"

She finished her glass of wine. "I think it's a Italian guy named Angelo, but that's all I know about him. Never seen him, don't know what he looks like. Never made no difference to me; I don't even see Sharkey but once in a while."

Angelo, thought Tony. Angelo. He'd heard that name. He sat quietly for a moment, frowning, scratched his thick thatch of wavy black hair. Suddenly it came to him. Back when he'd been about thirteen he'd known an older man—a guy about thirty or so then, named Chuck Swan, and they'd been about as friendly as two males of such dissimilar ages can get. Tony had been a hustling kid, wherever a fast buck was concerned, and Swan had used him fifteen or twenty times to do little jobs for him, especially jobs that a kid could do better than a grown-up. Tony had run errands, carried messages and packages without ever knowing the contents; he'd even pushed some queer ten-dollar bills that Swan supplied him with—for a dime a bill. Swan had taken Tony riding in his big new car, bought him a beer once in a while. He'd been mixed up in the rackets, always had a thick wad of money, and Tony liked being around the guy. Then Swan had dropped some hints that he was "moving up," and had mentioned this Angelo. Angelo was way up there sitting on top of the rackets, and he was setting up some sort of deal for Swan. Right after that Swan had left the neighborhood and Tony had never seen him again.

Tony thought about things Swan had told him, and his references to Angelo, and asked Maria, "This Angelo guy, he's about the biggest joe in the Frisco rackets, isn't he?"

"I dunno. He's pretty big, I guess."

"He tied in with any higher-ups? You know, the national guys?"

"They got the gambling, naturally, and the dope. But the girls is what you might call independent. Angelo's the whole thing far as Frisco is concerned—I mean that's as far as the girls' money goes."

"Must add up to dough," Tony said thoughtfully.

She lived in an apartment building up on Pine Street, out about a mile, and as they drove down Pine where the lights were a little dimmer than downtown, Tony put his arm around Maria's shoulder and pulled her to him. She lifted her head to look at him from inches away, and he pulled her closer, bending his face to hers.

This had to be right, he thought. She'd been slobbered on by enough drunken suckers and guys with only one thing on their minds. That wasn't the way to act around a woman, even a woman you were paying. Tony pulled Maria close to him, and he said softly, "You won't never get away from me again for no three years. I'm sure glad I found you again, Maria."

She said, "Oh, Tony, so'm I."

Then he kissed her. He kissed her softly with parted lips, gently, with no passion, no roughness, but almost with tenderness. He pulled her nearer to him, shifted in the back seat of the taxi so that their bodies were closer together, touching along more of their surfaces, and he pulled her tighter with his strong arms. His right hand caressed her shoulder, slid down her back, came to rest beneath her armpit at the swell of her breast. He kissed her carefully. And all the time his brain was coldly clicking, clicking, adding, multiplying, piling dollar upon dollar in his mind, and as if his eyes were turned inward upon his brain he saw the money growing, dollar upon dollar, pile upon pile, money, dollars, power.

Their lips parted with a soft moist sound and Maria leaned her head forward, burrowing it against his neck. "Oh, Tony, Tony," she whispered. He could feel the rise and fall of her breasts, hear the heavy breath sigh in and out of her throat.

"Maria, honey," he said. "Maria, baby."

They sat quietly for a few blocks, then she moved away from him. "We're almost there," she said. "You comin' up for a drink?"

"Sure."

"I got wine, Tony, good red wine, the kind you like. And I got gin and some whiskey."

"Swell, baby. Sounds real good."

Tony leaned back against the cushions and sighed. After a few seconds he asked pleasantly, "Say, honey. How many girls they got in that place on Fillmore?"

Chapter Two

Tony had a date to meet Maria at Pandy-Andy's on Maiden Lane about one in the morning, and he was getting cleaned up early Saturday night. He thought he'd walk around a little bit, maybe hang around the St. Francis or Union Square, a couple blocks from Pandy-Andy's, then have a drink or two to kill time.

He finished bathing and shaving in the bathroom, then walked back down the hall to his room. He'd run a comb through his thick black mass of wavy hair and was getting dressed in a dark blue single-breasted suit when the phone rang. It was Maria.

"Tony?"

"Yeah, honey. Who else you think'd be here?"

She laughed, then said, "Tony, I'm sorry, but I can't meet you at one. Something's come up."

"The hell. Christ, I'm already gettin' dressed up. What's the matter?"

"I got to go to a party. It's a real good thing for me—it's up at Sharkey's. You know, I mentioned him, he's one of the big fellows. I'm lucky to get to go, Tony. There's going to be four of us girls there, and Castiglio —he's Sharkey's man that's got my district—told me they wanted the prettiest girls, and *I'm* supposed to be one of them." She sounded excited, a bit breathless. She paused a moment, then said, "That's a real compliment, huh? Tony, you think I'm one of the prettiest?"

"You're the top, baby." Then he added, "Hell, Maria, I was lookin' forward to seein' you tonight. This a private party, or is there a chance I could run up after a while?"

"Look, hon, I gotta hurry. I got to get ready. About the party, it's more an open house thing, but just for the fellows work with Sharkey. There's Castiglio and another of the guys under him—"

"Angelo gonna be there?"

"No, just some of the guys. Castiglio tells me it's mainly for this Senator that's back in town."

"Jesus, a Congressman?"

"No, the state thing, what you call it?"

"Legislature?"

"Yeah. This Swan guy, Angelo's man. He's—"

"Who? Swan what? I mean what Swan? What's his first name?"

"I dunno. Just Swan. He's a good friend with Angelo."

"Jesus Christ, honey, I know the guy. He's a pal of mine—he was. Look, I want to go to that party." Tony's mind was busy; this was what he'd been waiting for. He could have gone to see Sharkey, even Angelo, and asked for a spot, any kind of spot in the organization —and probably he'd have gotten nowhere. This was perfect, better than he'd hoped, but it was like any break that ever was: A guy had to help make his own.

Maria said, "I know why you want to go there. You don't want to be with me; you want to meet those guys, Sharkey and the others."

She did know, of course; Tony had talked to her about wanting to get in with them, but Maria hadn't ever liked the idea. She wanted him to keep out of the racket, get in something else; she liked things just as they were between the two of them.

Tony said, "O.K., so I want to meet Sharkey. You can fix it for me."

"But I don't even know him, hon. Please. You don't want to come up. I'll see you after."

"You're goddamn right I want to come up. Now, you fix it."

"No, Tony."

"O.K., baby. You can get lost. I'll see you around."

He stopped, but held the receiver to his ear, listening. He *had* to get up to Sharkey's.

"Tony? You still there?"

"Yeah."

"Honey, I don't know how. I don't mean a thing to them guys."

"You don't have to. You go on up—when you supposed to be there?"

"Ten o'clock. About an hour from now."

"O.K. You'll meet Swan there. Tell him you know Tony Romero—just talked to him. Tell him I'm dyin' to see my old pal again. See? He can fix it easy; you tell him I want to come up there and see him. Up *there*."

"Well…all right, Tony." She sounded subdued, not as breathless and excited as she had been. "I'll do it, but maybe it won't make no difference."

"That's O.K. You just do it. And, baby, I won't mess you up none. I want to see Swan again—and talk to Sharkey a little. I won't get you in dutch."

"All right, Tony. I'll call you sometime after I get there."

"So long, baby. You call me."

He hung up and started walking back and forth in the small room. He smacked his big fist into his palm, brows furrowed. Hell, it couldn't miss, not if Swan was up there. Swan! How do you like that? Swan, of all people. The least the guy could do would be to get in touch with him. And Maria had said Swan was thick with Angelo. Angelo, the Top. Goddamn! This was it, all right. He couldn't miss now. Just that first little break was all a guy like Tony Romero needed, and this was the break. He pounded his palm again, rapidly, nervous and tense. He looked at his watch; only a few minutes past nine, over an hour till the brawl started. He had a light, excited feeling in his chest. Maybe in a little over an hour he'd be talking to the big boys, the real ones.

At ten minutes before eleven P.M. Tony walked over to the dresser, unknotted his tie and carefully tied it again, working the big knot up between the wide wings of his collar. He looked good. The suit had set him back a bill and a quarter to have made. It set well on his heavy shoulders, tapered smoothly to his lean, flat waist and hips. The dark blue looked all right on him too, with his dark complexion. He looked like a guy that knew his way around. He went back and sat down on the bed, lit the last cigarette in his pack and puffed nervously on it as he glanced at the phone. What the hell was wrong? He'd been sitting here for almost two hours now. If that Maria crossed him, he'd knock her silly. She didn't know how important this was to him; or maybe she did. Maybe that guy Swan was somebody else besides the one he'd known. Christ, he couldn't see Swan as a State Senator, anyway. That was it. He'd got himself all worked up for nothing. But Swan was the type: tall, blond, honest-looking guy, open-faced. And he had the voice for it, he remembered. Christ, he knew Angelo, though; it could be. Angelo could get damn near anybody in the goddamn legislature. Sonofabitch. He wanted a drink. A big drink. But if he went up to Sharkey's he wanted to be sober. There'd be plenty to drink up there. Goddamn, goddamn, goddamn. The hell with it. I'll get plastered. I'll make it another way. He stubbed out the cigarette after two deep drags, reached for the empty pack, fumbled inside it, then crumpled the pack and threw it into the corner.

The phone rang.

Tony jumped toward it, reached for it, then hesitated, let the phone ring again, a third time, before he picked up the receiver and said into the mouthpiece, "Hello.

It wasn't Maria. It was a man's voice, a deep, booming, pleasant voice. It was heavier, richer now, but it was the one he remembered. "Hey, Romero? This that punk kid, Tony?"

"Yeah. Swan? That you, Swan?"

"Himself. How are you, Tony? Where the hell you been, kid?"

"In Frisco all the time, Swan. Christ, you're doin' all right I hear. Man, it's sure good to hear you again. I ain't passed no queer for years. Times is tough."

Swan laughed. "I bet you're doing O.K., Tony. You always were a hot one."

"Well, not bad. You give me my start. Man, I'd sure like to see you again."

"Look, kid. I got a blonde hanging on my tail. I'll see you when you get up here."

Tony's heart thudded once, then beat normally. His mouth was dry and it seemed silly; he'd wanted to go up there more than he'd admitted even to himself. He said, "Up there? O.K. if I bust in, huh?"

"Why not? I'd like to shoot the breeze with you

again, kid. You always gave me a charge. Hell, this is just a loose brawl, anyway. Well, I gotta ring off. I'll see you.'

"Sure, Swan." Tony started to hang up, then remembered, panicked, that he didn't know where the party was. "Swan," he yelled into the mouthpiece. "Hey, *Swan.*"

"Yeah?"

"Hey, where you at? I almost forgot."

Swan laughed, then gave Tony the address and apartment number and hung up.

Even before he reached the door and rang the buzzer, Tony could hear the laughter and shrieks from inside the room. He was already a little awed by the place. Sharkey lived in the Arlington Arms, a big apartment house near the Bay. There was even one of those cloth canopy things over the walk leading up to the door, and when the cab had stopped a uniformed doorman had opened the door for Tony. Tony gave him a buck, then wondered what he'd done that for. There was sure no work to opening a door; he could do it for himself. The hell with it. He'd have to get used to giving out bucks to all the guys with palms shoved out, and a lofty air as if their crap smelled like Chanel.

He walked boldly through the rich lobby and took the elevator up to ten, then walked over thick carpeting to 1048. He rang the buzzer thinking that this was one of those places that smelled like money, smelled good, rich. It made him think of fat guys getting their pink faces patted in barber shops, and slant-eyed women with gold douche bags. He heard footsteps trotting toward the door and then the door swung open.

There was a slinky-looking, shapely brunette, almost as tall as Tony, standing inside holding the door open. Tony nodded at her, not sure what to say.

"Well!" she said. "Where'd you come from?" She raised one dark, thinly penciled eyebrow a half inch.

"I'm Tony Romero," he said. "Swan invited me up here."

"Well, come on in, honey."

Tony looked into the room as he brushed past the brunette. She shut the door behind him and he pressed his teeth together, feeling good, enjoying himself already, glancing rapidly around the room and taking it all in, drinking it in. This was something. He was in the big living room and it was the room that Tony had half visualized in his mind, the room he wanted. There was even a bar against one wall, four chrome-and-red-leather stools in front of it; on the opposite wall was a huge picture five or six feet square, of half a dozen nude women running around in a kind of mist in green forest by a lake, some of them swimming.

There were twelve or fifteen people in the living loom, and he could hear more voices from the open door of the kitchen ahead and on his right. Noise and laughter and conversation beat against his ears and he could smell the odor of whiskey cutting sharply through the faint scent of women, of their bodies and their perfume. Three people sat on a long divan, all of them holding highballs, others were at the bar, and some stood about the room, talking and drinking. Directly ahead of him, across the room from the entrance, the wall was a huge window, black draperies at each side. It was night beyond the window, but Tony knew the Bay was out there, and the lights of the Golden Gate and the San Francisco Bay Bridge.

He sucked in his breath, glancing rapidly about. He hadn't yet recognized anyone; the few seconds he had stood inside the door had been filled only with the sudden impact of sound and color and the heavy and subtle odors. He heard Swan's booming laugh and spotted him, tall and blond, leaning against the wall on the right of the black drapery at the window's edge. He was talking to a red-haired woman who played with the ribbed lapel of his dinner jacket.

Tony walked toward him just as Swan looked around and saw him. "Hi, kid," he boomed, and advanced toward Tony with one hand extended. They met in the middle of the room and shook hands. Tony felt swell. Several of those in the room turned to look at them; at Tony Romero in this swank place shaking hands with Swan—with *State Senator* Swan.

"Hello, Swan," Tony said. "Sure good to see you. Or maybe I should call you Mr. Swan, or The Honorable something, or whatever it is."

"It's Swan, kid. Same old bastard." He looked Tony up and down. "Jesus. You've grown up into a little mountain. What you weigh now?"

"About one-eighty."

"Let's see, you're—twenty now, huh?"

Tony grinned. "Well...twenty-three. No, make it twenty-two."

"You sonofabitch," Swan grinned, "You haven't changed," He jerked his head. "Come on, I'll introduce you to Shark."

"Sure." This was just as good as if he'd planned it himself. Swan put his hand on Tony's shoulder and steered him across the room to where a solidly built man sat in a low, wide, cream-colored chair. Maria sat on the arm of the chair talking to the guy. Swan took Tony up to them and stopped.

So this was Sharkey? He was a big egg, about as tall as Swan, thicker through the chest and middle. He looked around forty, with a pouchy, lined face and a bald spot in the middle of his head. The face was square, with the thick-lipped mouth a straight line gashing the face, the lips almost too red. What hair he had left was red, too, more pinkish than anything else. One of Sharkey's chunky hands rested on Maria's thigh, a stubble of short, thick red hairs on the back of his hand like a week-old beard.

With a slight shock Tony noticed that Sharkey was drunk. He didn't know why he should have been shocked or surprised; everybody was drinking and it seemed to be a pretty wild party. It just didn't seem right that a big shot like Sharkey would be plastered. Swan had obviously been drinking quite a bit, too, but it didn't show much. He just seemed to be having a hell of a good time.

Tony looked at Maria. He didn't know whether he should say hello or not; he hadn't thought about it before. But she smiled and said, "Hello, Tony," when he and Swan walked up.

He winked at her. "Hi, Maria."

Swan said, "Hey, Shark. Look alive. Here's the kid I was telling you about. Tony Romero. Tony, this is Al Sharkey."

"Pleased to meet you, Mr. Sharkey," said Tony. "I heard a lot about you."

Sharkey looked up and smacked his lips. "Romero, huh?" He blinked pale blue eyes. His eyes were too small, Tony thought. Didn't look big enough in that square face, and they looked bloodshot. No good reason, but he didn't like Sharkey's looks. Sharkey went on, "Swanney tells me you're a regular piss-cutter. That right?"

"Well…" said Tony. Jesus. What kind of question was that? Was the guy making fun of him? And what the hell was a piss-cutter, anyway? Was that good? "I known Mr. Swan quite a while," he said.

Sharkey nodded. "Well, glad to know you, Romero. Make yourself at home. Have a drink, boy. And, say, how about bringing me a whiskey-coke while you're at it. My feet hurt."

For a moment irritation flared in Tony. He wasn't no goddamn servant. But he fought the anger down, forced himself to take it easy, and said, "Sure, Mr. Sharkey. Just a minute."

Swan took over then. "Hey, Ginny," he yelled toward the bar. "Bring us a coke-high and—" he looked at Tony. "What you want?"

"What you drinking?"

"Scotch and water."

"Me too, then."

Swan laughed and slapped his hip. "You little son-ofabitch. If I said poison, I bet *you'd* say poison." He asked Maria what she wanted then yelled, "Ginny, and two scotch-and-waters and a rum-coke. O.K., honey?"

The brunette who'd let Tony in waved a hand and started mixing the drinks. Sharkey slid his hand along Maria's green skirt and squeezed her thigh. She glanced at Tony, then put her hand over Sharkey's and patted it. When the drinks came, Swan steered Tony over to the window and pulled two chairs together facing the view. Tony sat down and looked out over the Bay.

They talked casually for a few minutes, finished their drinks. Swan told him that he'd known Angelo well even before he'd first run into Tony; they were good friends, "like that." Angelo had fixed Swan up for the legislature job where he could look out for Angelo's interests. Yeah, Angelo was The Top, for sure. He had all the gambling, dope, houses, the works. He was tied in with the national bunch on the rest, but the houses were his, independent. Of course Angelo had his fingers in a lot of legit things too—that was mainly where Swan came in—apartment houses, this one here for example, a couple movie houses, some other real estate and pieces of several nightclubs. Yeah, he must be worth a million or two. Maybe more. Finally Swan asked Tony what he'd been doing, how he'd been getting along.

Tony hesitated for a moment, then he said, "Hell, I'll tell you the truth, Swan. I'm not doing much of anything right now. I pick up enough to get by, but no big dough." He paused. "Christ, I'd give a nut to get in with these guys." He jerked his head toward the room behind him. "Sharkey, and the rest."

"What you want in with them for, kid? Why this racket? There's better spots."

"There's reasons. I could do good in this one. And there's big money in it. I thought a lot about it."

Swan nodded. "I'll bet you have." He grinned. "I suppose you want me to put in a word for you, huh?"

"Well, no, Swan. I mean—"

"The hell. That's why you came up here, isn't it? Don't forget, I know you, kid. Unless you've changed a lot, and I'll give you odds you haven't."

"I came up to see you, Swan. But it sure wouldn't hurt me none if you put in a word for me." Tony squinted at the other. "Dammit, I want in. I want in." His voice was suddenly tighter. "I got to get started, Swan. A guy don't live forever."

Swan laughed. "What a way for a twenty-year-old kid to talk. Pardon me, Tony, a twenty-two-year-old kid. But you might do O.K. at that. But take a tip. Seriously. Don't try to go too fast; that's your trouble. And it can get you plenty grief. I know; I've seen it happen too often."

Tony turned the empty glass in his fingers, shook the small piece of ice left in the glass, then he looked up. "Swan," he said soberly, "a guy like me can't go too fast."

Swan looked back at him, chewing on his lip. He shook his head. "You're wrong, Tony. But I'll see what the score is. There's one guy Sharkey's having trouble with. Shark's got three men directly under him that handle the actual business of running the houses, report to him, turn in the collections and so on. There's Castiglio and Hamlin and Alterie, Frank Alterie. It's Alterie that isn't getting along with Shark;

and there's talk he's on the needle. Maybe there's nothing there, but I'll see." He sighed and got up. "Well, I better mingle a little. You might as well roam around and get acquainted. Drinks are free."

"Yeah." Involuntarily Tony glanced at Sharkey, now tilting another glass to his red lips and gulping from it.

Swan followed his gaze and said pleasantly, "Well, it's his liquor, kid."

"He seems to like it. Who's who around here? I mean with the houses."

Swan pointed out Hamlin and Castiglio, and a third man he knew only as Beezer. Alterie wasn't present. There were others, but Tony was mainly interested in Castiglio at the moment. He was a short, dark, thin-faced Italian about twenty-five, wearing a double-breasted brown suit with small checks in the cloth. He was sitting in a wide leather chair, and the girl who had met Tony at the door—Ginny, Swan had called her— was sitting on his lap. Tony walked past them, then stopped and looked around. He nodded to Castiglio, started to walk away, then turned. "Say," he said, "can I get you two anything to drink?"

"Well, thanks," Castiglio said. "I could use a shot of that Granddad with a water chaser." He glanced at Ginny on his lap, then grinned at Tony. "Fix it myself, but I hate to get up."

Tony grinned at him. "Don't blame you. How about you?" He looked at the woman.

"You know how to mix a stinger?"

"Not exactly."

"You either know exactly, or you don't know at all."

"O.K. I don't know at all."

She laughed and told him how to mix the drink. Then, while Tony was still watching, she turned to Castiglio, put her face close to his, and slid her tongue out between her teeth. Castiglio kissed her tongue, then sort of slid his mouth up it till he was kissing her lips; one hand eased up the front of her dress. Tony was getting hotter than hell. Tony thought it was time he got behind the bar.

Behind the bar he found the white Creme de Menthe and the brandy, stirred it in cracked ice and found a glass that looked delicate enough for such a foolish drink, then made Castiglio's and his own. He mentally imagined himself chopping wood for a few seconds, until he cooled down a little and figured it was safe to walk across the room again, then put the drinks on a tray and took them back to the other two.

Ginny tasted her stinger and pursed her lips. "Very good for an amateur," she said.

"Thanks."

"Oh," she said. "You two don't know each other." She looked up at Tony. "By the way, what's your name?"

"Tony Romero."

"Tony, this is Leo Castiglio."

"Hi, Tony." Castiglio stuck out his hand and Tony shook it, making sure it was a firm, hearty handshake. "Glad to know you, Mr. Castiglio," he said.

"Jesus, it's Leo. Nobody calls me Mr. Castiglio but the draft board."

"Don't you want to know who I am?" she asked.

"I heard Swan call you Ginny."

"Short for Virginia." She laughed. "I know, I know, but I was never called Virgin for short. What do you say we dance, Tony?"

"Well…"

"Oh, come on."

Tony looked down at Leo Castiglio. "You mind?"

"Hell, no," he said, and Ginny, for no good reason that Tony could figure out, started laughing so hard she almost choked.

She got off Leo's lap, smoothed her dress, then held her hands out toward Tony and he stepped toward her. The record on now was a slow fox trot, and Tony put his arm around her and took her left hand in his. She was a good, smooth dancer, and she danced close to him, following him easily. At first they didn't talk, then she asked him, "Having fun?"

"Sure am. This is a swell party, huh?"

"That it is. I'll have to work on Al to have more of them. If you'll come. Will you, Tony?"

He didn't answer right away. Al? Oh, yeah, Al Sharkey. What'd she mean, work on him?

"You mean Mr. Sharkey? You know him pretty well?"

She laughed again. "*Know* him! Good Lord, we've been married for six years."

Tony missed a step. If she kept surprising him like this he wasn't going to be able to take a step without missing a step. "Married?" he said. "Married?"

"Well," she smiled, "what's wrong with that? We... understand each other."

Tony looked over her shoulder to where he'd last seen Sharkey. The chair was empty now and he looked around. Then he spotted Sharkey sitting at the bar with a girl. Maria was sitting on the divan with Swan now. Some of the faces he'd seen earlier weren't in sight, but nobody had left. He remembered then that he'd noticed a couple other doors leading into bedrooms. Christ, this was some party. Maybe it was a little strange, but this was sure the life, thought Tony.

He said, "Nothing wrong with it at all, Mrs. Sharkey." She frowned and he said, "Ginny, I mean. It just surprised me. I mean I didn't expect it."

"Well, don't worry about it, Tony. I like the way you dance."

The way she was dancing, Tony thought he should still be behind the bar. But he said, "You're a swell dancer, Ginny. I hope Mr. Sharkey—I mean, I sure don't want him mad at me. I been hoping I could go to work for him maybe."

"Oh? Then you'd have to come to all his parties, wouldn't you?"

He grinned at her then, pulled her a little tighter to him. The hell with going behind the bar; let her know how he felt, and see what happened. Sharkey's wife, huh? He held her tightly against him as they moved slowly over the floor and said, "I'd have to. He'd be the boss. Can't think of anything I'd like more—coming to his parties, I mean."

"Have you talked to him?"

"Not yet. I...don't want to rush things."

She smiled at that and was still smiling as the dance ended. As they dipped on the last note of music, she followed close to him, molded her body to his as she looked into his face still smiling. She squirmed her loins against him, briefly, and said, "Why not rush things?"

He licked his lips. "Why not?" he said. He glanced at Sharkey, sitting at the bar with his back to them, and then as he released her he let his hand glide down the smooth fabric of her dress and over the swell of her hip, lingering just a moment on its softness before he dropped his hand to his side.

She took his hand and pulled him to the chair in which Castiglio had been sitting. He was dancing with another girl now. Tony sat down and Ginny eased onto his lap.

She smiled. Her fingers unbuttoned his shirt and

slid inside against his skin, the nails digging gently into him, "Do you like me, Tony?"

"Sure. Too much." He glanced at Sharkey.

"Don't worry about him." Her face slowly grew more sober, tense-looking and she took his right hand in her free hand. She slid it toward her, up her thigh and pressed it against her stomach, looking at his mouth all the time. He moved his fingers slightly, and she smiled with her lips pressed against her teeth, then pulled his hand up to the V of her dress and inside. He put his other arm around her and pulled her to him.

Hell, he thought, a guy had to take a chance, and she was a hot one. She couldn't be much more than twenty-five or twenty-six, and she was built like a burlesque stripper. He pulled his mouth from hers and looked around. Nobody was paying any attention to them.

She said softly, "Still like me, Tony?"

"Better every minute." He paused. "I don't think I'll head to L.A. Not for a while."

"I'll talk to Al. I'd like for you to stick around a while, honey. You like that?"

"You damn bet I'd like that."

"All right; let's not talk about it any more. Tony, honey, honey, give me another one of those nice kisses."

"Just a minute." Sharkey had got up from the bar and Tony watched him walk unsteadily to a chair. He plopped down into it heavily, and his head fell back on the cushion behind him.

Ginny looked at him and said softly to Tony, "He's through. About every other party this happens. I know him like a book. Watch his drink."

Tony didn't get what she meant, but he kept looking at Sharkey. In a minute or two the glass that Sharkey held in his hand tilted and the drink spilled out onto his trousers. The glass fell from his fingers and stopped between his leg and the padded chair arm. He lay quietly, breathing through his open mouth.

Tony looked around the room. Two couples were wound together on the couch and others were in the wide chairs. He didn't see Maria. He could hear soft voices from the kitchen, but it was quiet in the living room now except for soft music from the record player.

"Sort of cleared out," Tony said.

"Uh-huh. The living room clears out and the bed-rooms fill up. Too rich for your blood?"

"No. I like it. Just the way it is."

He kissed her, pulled her tightly against him. His heart was beginning to pound heavily, and he slid his arms around her and jerked her roughly to him, squeezing her, holding her tight.

She pulled her mouth from his and kissed his cheek and throat, whispering. "God, you're strong. You hurt me, Tony, but it's all right, it's all right. You're strong, honey, and I like it. I like you strong." Her lips caressed his cheek and moved toward his mouth as she said, the words muffled, "Hold me like that, Tony, honey, hold me hard like that."

In a minute she slid from his lap, walked to the door and flipped the light switch in the wall and the room was dark with black darkness. Then she was back. She sat on his lap again, facing him, one knee on each side of his body in the space between the chair arms and his legs. She put one hand on each side of his face, moved toward him and kissed him hungrily, holding his face in her hands.

He felt shaky. He'd been with many women, but this Ginny was doing something to him, getting under his skin. It felt as if his heart were pounding all through his body and his skin burned where she touched him. One of her hands left his face and crept inside his shirt, slid up and down on his bare stomach. He put his hands behind her waist and pulled her closer to him, and she reached to the top of her dress, pulled it from her shoulders, then put his hands on her skin, moving against him. She leaned close and whispered to him, kissing his lips and cheeks with light, quick kisses.

He said softly, "You mean it?"

"Yes." Her voice was shaking, "Here. Now, honey."

"I...don't know."

"*Yes!* Damn it, yes." Then her lips were on his again, and her hands fumbled, touched him, and she moved slowly, smoothly against him.

Chapter Three

Walking back to his hotel at three o'clock the following afternoon, Tony felt good. He had Swan on his side, Ginny working for him, and now, after a few friendly beers with Leo, it looked as though he might help a little, too. Tony knew more now about the trouble between Sharkey and Alterie. Alterie was paying too much attention to his girls, and women outside the houses; that wasn't so bad in itself, but at the same time he was paying too little attention to business. It wasn't known for sure that he was on dope, but he'd been increasingly short-tempered and irritable the past months.

Tony had been interested to learn that of the three "districts," Alterie controlled the one which included the area Tony was most familiar with: a big, lopsided triangle bordered on one side by Market, on the other by Army Street, and with the Bay and Embarcadero as its base. It included Howard Street where Tony had been born and had grown up; Harrison and Mission where he'd played and where some of his friends had lived; the numbered streets from First to Twenty-Sixth, Brannon, Division, Fremont, Portrero; it included Seal Stadium where he'd rooted loudly for the Seals;

and it included the San Francisco Emergency Hospital where many of Tony's friends, and enemies, had spent some time.

Leo Castiglio had the downtown district on the other side of Market, extending out as far as Masonic and Presidio Avenues, including Fillmore and the house Maria was in. He also handled, with Sharkey, the call girl racket which was spreading faster than the houses themselves. All the other scattered houses were under Hamlin. Alterie's district was between the other two in area, but did a lot of business and accounted for more than a third of the revenue from the houses themselves.

In his hotel room, Tony lay on the bed and stared at the ceiling, not seeing it. Leo had invited Tony to lunch again the next day—on Leo this time. Tony grinned, thinking to himself that Leo was going to be easy.

He thought about the money in the racket. He still didn't know exactly how many houses there were in Frisco, but judging by Leo's conversation there must be a hundred spots or more. Tony played with figures in his head and after a few minutes he was dizzy. That, he thought, was *dough*.

Ginny called him ten days later. It was about eleven o'clock Thursday morning, and Tony had just climbed out of bed in his hotel room. He was dressed and leaving for breakfast when the phone rang. He answered it.

"Tony?"

"Uh-huh. Who's this?"

"Well, who do you think?"

"Hell, I don't know," he said pleasantly. "So many dames always callin' me up...hi, Ginny. How are you?"

"Well, that's better. I was ready to hang up. And after I've been fixing things for you, too."

Tony's interest quickened. "You mean I can start to work? Am I in?"

He heard her sigh over the phone. "You Tony. Sure, starting tomorrow you're first assistant to Charlie Lucky. Relax, will you? I just thought I'd tell you Al wants to see you this afternoon."

"Yeah? When?"

"Four o'clock."

"Swell. He gonna look at me or give me a job?"

"Tony, sometimes—you'll either go a long way or get yourself killed in a hurry. You ever say thanks? Al wants to talk to you; probably he'll find something for you to do—like carrying pans of water to the girls. But promise me something."

"Sure."

"Don't ask Al for *his* job this afternoon."

He laughed. "O.K. I'll wait a while. Hey, when am I gonna see you again? It's been a couple weeks almost."

"You *do* want to see me then?"

"What you think's been keeping me awake nights?"

"Some redhead, probably. I thought maybe you were being nice to me so I'd talk to Al."

"I was, you guessed it. But now you've talked to him, let's switch it. You be nice to me."

"One o'clock, Tony?"

"Where?"

"Your place."

"It's not very fancy," he said.

"It's got a bed, hasn't it?"

"Yeah, honey, it's got a bed."

Tony glanced at his watch as he rode up in the elevator. One minute till four. He'd press the buzzer at exactly four P.M. He felt a little tense and nervous, even though Ginny had told him that Al was ready to try him out in a small way, see how he got along with the boys and madams and girls—and with Al Sharkey, himself—test him out a little. That was all Tony asked: a foot in the door. He'd bust the door in to get the rest of the way, if he had to.

He was glad Ginny had showed up at one, though, and told him Al's mind was already about made up. Should make the coming interview easier. It had been a pleasant couple of hours they'd spent together, too.

Tony left the elevator and walked to 1048. Ginny should be home by now; she'd left at three o'clock and come back here after the "show" she'd gone to. Funny thing about the Shark; he didn't care if his wife did the dance of no veils at the parties—when he was occupied, himself—but he didn't want her chasing around behind his back as he put it. The jerk.

The door opened and Ginny stood there. "Well, Tony!" she said. "It's good to see you again after all this time. Come in."

He looked past her, anxiously, but Sharkey wasn't in sight. "I been busy," he said, and walked inside.

She grinned. "Al's waiting for you in his office. I'll take you in."

He followed her through one of the bedrooms on the right, and through it into a small room. Sharkey sat at a small black desk facing a window that looked out to the Bay. There were two overstuffed chairs in the room besides the leather one he sat in. On the wall beyond him was a framed painting of red swirls and yellow blobs and violet lines. It didn't make sense to Tony, but it was in an expensive-looking gold frame. There was a gray carpet covering the floor of Sharkey's office. Pretty nice place, thought Tony.

Ginny said, "Here he is, Al, honey. Tell him all about sin." She went out and shut the door.

Sharkey turned more toward Tony and looped a heavy leg over his chair arm. "Hello, Romero. Sit down." He nodded toward a chair near the desk.

Tony said hello and sat down, crossed his legs and

looked at Sharkey. He was sober; Tony wondered if the guy actually remembered him. He didn't look much better sober. His lips were still too straight and red, and his hair was still that sad pinkish color, and mostly gone.

Sharkey looked at Tony for a few seconds without speaking, lips pursed. He said, "You'd like it if I give you a job, huh?"

"Well...I'd like it a lot, Mr. Sharkey. I'd like to work for you."

"Why'd you like to work for me?"

The bastard, why didn't he talk sensible? Tony said, "Well, I heard you're a good guy to work for, and..." He stopped. "Hell," he said, "main reason is dough. I want to make dough, Mr. Sharkey—I'd like to have a place like you got here, say. Real Class. I think I could do good for you. I don't care what kind of work you give me—if you do. But I want to get started."

He figured he'd said enough and shut up. Sharkey looked at him for a while, frowning, then he said, "What the hell are you, Romero, some kind of genius or something? Or are you just nosy?"

Tony felt himself getting angry. This Sharkey rubbed him the wrong way. He'd like to stand up and slug the guy one in the middle of those red lips. He swallowed and said, "I don't think I know what you mean."

"I'll tell you. First Swan comes and puts a bug in my

ear. Romero. Regular piss-cutter. Then Ginny says I ought to give a ambitious kid like you a tryout. Then, by God, Leo bends my ear. Romero. He's a fine fellow, this Romero. You been a pretty busy kid, huh?"

Tony had to suppress a smile. Those half dozen lunches and talks with Castiglio had paid off, too. Well, hell, a guy had to help make his breaks. He and Leo were pretty chummy now. They'd talked quite a bit about what Tony might be able to start out doing.

Tony said, "Yeah, I seen quite a lot of Leo. He's a swell guy. That's another reason I'd like workin' for you—Leo says you're a real good guy to work for." Leo hadn't said any such thing, but Sharkey looked pleased for a moment.

"He did, huh?"

"He sure did. Leo and I get along good. He says he didn't know anyone he'd rather work for. Well, he kind of got me thinking that way, too."

Sharkey nodded. Then he said, "Say, kid, you like a drink?"

Tony hesitated only a moment. He didn't want to get off on the wrong foot, but it didn't seem like you could get off on the wrong foot by having a drink with this egg. He smiled. "Well, thanks. I wouldn't mind a small one. I seen your bar out there when I was up Saturday. That's really it."

Sharkey raised his voice and yelled, "Ginny! Hey, Ginny!"

She came in and Sharkey told her to mix a couple drinks for him and the kid.

Ginny said, "And one for me. Well, Mr. Romero, you a pimp yet?"

"Oh, for Christ's sake," Sharkey said. "You and your goddamn mouth."

She laughed and went out, returning in a couple minutes with the drinks. She sat down while Sharkey talked to Tony and guzzled his highball. "Tell you what, Romero. You're so all-fired dyin' to work, I'm gonna let you work a little. You go around with Leo tonight. He's going to some of the houses; you go along. I ain't going to pay you nothing for anything. Leo, he'll have a few things for you to do. You do what he says."

"Glad to, Mr. Sharkey. And I appreciate the chance to start in. Anything at all's fine with me."

Sharkey finished his drink and turned to Ginny. "Mix me another—put some pep in it this time." Then he said to Tony, "You work out O.K., you'll go on a little salary. Well, that's all. I got to get to work."

Tony stood up. He figured Sharkey had to get to work on a bottle. "Thanks a lot, Mr. Sharkey," he said. "I appreciate it."

Sharkey nodded. Tony went out. Ginny was mixing a drink at the bar. He walked over to her, reached up and squeezed her waist, with his hand. "Thanks, sweetheart," he said softly. "I'm practically in business."

She smiled. "I'll give you a ring."

Tony grinned at her, didn't say anything, and left. Going down in the elevator he kept grinning to himself. It looked like he had that foot in the door. Now to start getting all the dope he could dig up on Frank Alterie.

Chapter Four

Frank Alterie was a pretty tough character but when he and Tony had their beefs Tony handled himself well enough.

Tony, of course, didn't know just how things were going to work out when he left Sharkey after that first talk and went back to his hotel, but he had plenty of confidence, and the conviction, even then, that he was on his way. He phoned Leo and arranged to meet him at seven o'clock that night for a drink in the St. Francis' Patent Leather Room, then they got into Leo's new Oldsmobile sedan and headed for the first stop.

Leo turned north on Van Ness and grinned at Tony. "Man," he said, "the first time I seen you up at Sharkey's, I never thought you'd be goin' around with me. What all did Shark say, anyhow?"

"Not much. Said you'd show me around, maybe have some things for me to do. Where we goin' now?"

"Big spot on Pacific. Got thirty ten-dollar girls there. See, Tony, I got forty spots; I pick up at eight of them a night, and two days I take off, don't do nothin'."

"You must handle plenty cash, Leo."

"Yeah. That's one reason I split up the houses for

five nights. Wouldn't want it all on me at once. Too many guys around here might feel like jumpin' me for it."

Tony thought about that, frowning. He hadn't considered this angle much before. "How much you think you'll wind up with tonight?" he asked.

Leo pulled a folded paper from his inside coat pocket and handed it to Tony. It listed eight locations and the amount to be picked up from each. After the address of the first house they were to visit was a figure: 124.

"What's this, Leo? What's that one-two-four?"

"Twelve thousand, four hundred. We pick up half that at the first house; there's amounts for the rest, too. See, Tony, them figures come through Sharkey—he gets the info from all the spots. They keep records, naturally, so Shark knows how much us guys pick up as the organization's cut."

"Jesus Christ," Tony said. "You get that much dough from this one place?"

"Sure, sixty-two-hundred, that's our fifty percent off the top. Figure it out. There's thirty ten-dollar girls there; that's half the gross through a whole week, through last night. Pretty good week, too."

Tony added the rest of the figures in his head, rapidly. "My God," he said. "You mean we'll wind up with over twenty-four thousand dollars tonight?"

"Twenty-four thousand, three-hundred clams."

"Sweet Jesus! What if some guy tries to beat you for it?"

"They got good sense, they won't try. All the guys in town know we're under Shark—and Angelo. And we got the right cops, too." Leo hesitated. "But in case some guy thinks it's a soft touch, we got these." He reached under his coat and then tossed something into Tony's lap.

Tony grabbed it, picked it up gingerly. It was a heavy .45 automatic and for a moment his throat closed up as he thought of what might happen if some guy jumped them for the dough. Then he swallowed and shrugged. Hell, this was part of it, and he'd never kidded himself that it wasn't. With that much money around a guy had to be able to take care of it.

It jarred Tony a little, though, to realize Leo was carrying a gun. He liked Leo. Tony had arranged to "bump into" Leo in the beginning for no other reason than to use him if he could; now he was starting to like the guy's company simply because he was pleasant to be around. But Tony had never realized the pleasant little guy packed a heater.

"Hey, Leo," he asked. "You ever have to use this thing?"

"I got jumped once. Single guy. I got out with the cash, though." He didn't say any more about it, but Tony saw him unconsciously reach up to the right edge of his jaw and stroke it a moment, then put his hand

back on the steering wheel. Tony had noticed a small
red scar there when he'd first met Leo, but he'd never
mentioned it. He didn't now. If Leo wanted to talk
about it, he would.

Tony rested his head against the seat behind him
thinking that tonight he was getting a different picture
of the business than he'd got from Maria. He asked
casually, "Any of the other guys ever get jumped?"

"Just Alterie once. Some guy sapped him and got
about thirty thou. Part was in checks—there's always
some checks."

"Guy get away with it?"

"Yeah." Leo pulled over to the curb and said, "First
stop, Tony. Come on."

They got out and walked up to the house. It was an
old, two-story place set back about forty feet off
Pacific, looking seventy or eighty years old. It looked
respectable enough, Tony thought. The place was dark,
as if somebody inside were sleeping. They walked up
the steps to the door and Leo rang. A Negro maid
opened the door and smiled when she saw who it was.

"Come on in, Mr. Leo. Ethel's waitin' for you."

They went inside, into a long hall stretching ahead
of them to the rear of the house. As they passed an
open door on their left Tony looked through it into a
large, well-furnished room in which two or three men
were sitting. A woman dressed only in a gray satin
housecoat sat on a couch beside a young man, her

hand resting on his knee. Tony got a glimpse of a couple other women in the room before he went on down the hall and into a small room on their right.

There were a couch and three chairs in the room, plus a dresser laden with cosmetics and perfumes. The room smelled sweet, almost sickening. Ethel, the landlady of the house, was a small woman who appeared almost fifty. Obviously she was the madam and not one of the girls. She had been sitting at the dressing table, peering into the mirror as she put black pencil on her brows, but she turned and got up as Leo and Tony came in.

"Leo, darling," she said, coming forward with her hand extended. "Still love me, dearie?"

"Sure," Leo grinned. He introduced Tony and Ethel and they shook hands. She had a strong grip, like a man's.

Ethel took a white envelope from the dresser and handed it to Leo. He sat down on the couch and pulled out a thick wad of bills and checks, then began counting the money, writing a few figures on the back of the envelope.

Tony watched him, a feverish feeling growing inside him as he stared at the money. Six-thousand, two-hundred dollars, he was thinking; the figure tumbled over and over in his mind. And that just half the dough from this one house. He thought hungrily about the huge, steady flow of dollars. In his mind grew an obscene image of a great fleshy whore lying on a bed, her legs parted and a constant stream of dollars spurting from her: dollar bills, ten-dollar bills, hundred- and thousand-dollar bills, filling the room, smothering her, flowing out of the doors and windows, a cascade, a flood, of money rushing day and night from the woman's thighs.

"O.K.," said Leo. He casually stuffed the money into the envelope, sealed it, and thrust it into his inside coat pocket. "Thanks, Ethel. See you next week. I'm going to show Tony around a little."

"Fine, Leo. Make yourselves right at home."

Leo grinned. "Don't worry."

They went out. Leo put his hand on Tony's shoulder and steered him toward the front of the house. "You know the setup," he said. "We passed the parlor when we come through. There's where the guys go when they come in. Any girls that ain't busy go in and the guy takes his pick—unless he asks for a certain dame. We got thirty rooms in this place so all the girls can work at once if it gets that jammed up."

Tony said, "How come you don't just send all that cabbage to the bank every day? Aren't you worried luggin' it all around?"

Leo grinned. "Bank? This don't go in no bank account, pal. I even burn this slip I got when I finish tonight."

They went into the parlor. It looked very much like

the large living room of an ordinary home. There were three big couches, some easy chairs, a table against the wall with some wilting chrysanthemums in it. It looked a bit dismal to Tony. There were four women in the room, scantily clad, and two men. As they entered one of the men went out through another door with a woman.

Tony and Leo sat on a couch and Tony said, "Seems like you could fix this place up some, Leo. You know, make it sharper, more sexy. Hell, that's what the guys come here for."

Leo said, "Don't worry, they'll come anyway. No need to spend dough makin' the place fancy." He grinned and tapped his coat over the fat envelope.

"Maybe so," Tony said, but he was thinking he'd make some changes if he were the boss.

The two unattached women walked toward them. One of them, a tall black-haired woman with thin, arched eyebrows and a full mouth said, "Hi, Leo. You miss me?"

"Sure, sweetheart, you know it." He pulled her down on his lap.

The other, a plump redhead, sat down by Tony and said, "You workin' with Leo, honey?"

"Yeah, in a way."

She smiled and rubbed his thigh with her hand. "Want to have a little fun?"

Tony looked at Leo, who was squeezing the other

woman, apparently in no hurry to leave. He heard the redhead and said to Tony, "Relax, pal. We got plenty time to hit the other places. Might as well enjoy the work, huh?" He laughed.

Tony shrugged. In a few minutes Leo got up and said, "Might as well kill a half hour, pal. I'm gonna be busy for that long." He looked from Tony to the red-head and grinned. "Won't cost him nothin', will it, Lou?"

" 'Course not, Leo. You know better'n that."

"Go ahead, Leo," Tony said. "I'll wait here for you."

"You kiddin'? Don't cost you nothin', Tony."

"I'll wait."

Leo shook his head, frowning, then he and the brunette went out of the room.

The redhead said, "What's the matter with you? Or is something wrong with me?"

"Nothing wrong with you, honey. I just don't mix business with pleasure." He grinned. "And it *would* be a pleasure."

The answer mollified her a little, but she said, "You don't know what you're missin', Tony." She paused. "Tony what?"

"Romero."

"You gonna be comin' round with Leo much?"

"Probably. I'll be seein' you."

"You do that." The doorbell rang and three men came in. The redhead looked up, then said to Tony,

"Well, honey, mama's got to get back to work. See you later."

"Sure."

Tony sat in the parlor for almost half an hour, waiting for Leo, and the time passed quickly as he watched the stream of men come in, and noted the way the girls operated. He hadn't been in a whorehouse for almost two years, and he'd forgotten how brusque and businesslike the whores had been in their advances. This house was a regular slot machine.

As he watched, a new arrival came in and sat down; one of the women sat beside him and ran her hand boldly up his thigh. It was a little too much like a set routine. Hell, everybody knew what the guys and gals were here for, but there wasn't any reason why it couldn't be handled with a little class. A little dough spent in the right places could turn this into one hell of a nice spot, too. The girls were all good-looking, a few of them actually beautiful, with full, soft bodies and striking faces. Tony watched the routine, and waited, with his mind busy.

When Leo came back he said, "You mean to tell me you been sittin' there since I left?"

"Yeah. Have a good time?"

Leo smacked his lips and rubbed his palms together. "Man, did I! What's the matter, you queer or something?"

Tony laughed. "Christ, no. But I'm afraid I'm gonna

be a disappointment to you, pal. I don't mean to mess with none of these women. I—" he paused for a moment, not wanting to get on the wrong side of Leo by saying he figured a guy was a sucker for messing with the whores he bossed; and that the fact that he was boss was just about the same as paying them the ten clams. The girls could hardly object, even if you made them sick, and Tony simply didn't care for sex on a platter.

Leo said, "You afraid of gettin' a dose?"

"No, that's not it exactly. Partly, maybe. But—I got me a girl takes good care of me, Leo. Maria Casino. She's out in your Fillmore spot."

"Oh, yeah. That sweet little chick." He shrugged. "Well, it's your business, kid. Sure nice stuff in here, though. Come on, then, let's go."

A little after two in the morning, Tony was talking to Maria in her apartment. She'd mixed a couple drinks for them and he'd just finished telling her about going around with Leo.

She frowned slightly. "Tony, I wish you'd stay out of it. What you want in this lousy racket for?"

"What's lousy about it? There's big dough in it, honey. And I mean to get me some of it. A lot of it."

"Tony...I do pretty good, you know it. I make enough for both of us. I wouldn't mind—"

He interrupted her, "Baby, I don't want no peanuts. I

want the big dough. You got any idea how much is in this racket? Must be at least ten, twenty million a year."

"I know, but Sharkey and Angelo get the most. You can't get nothin' except what they give you. And, honey, I don't like the guys in the racket. They're all sort of slimy guys. I don't want you to get like them. I like you just like you are, Tony."

"Oh, for Christ's sake, Maria. What you want me to do? Go into business with you muggin' guys in alleys? I got to get in someplace where I can move up, really make it. Well, this is it."

"Please, Tony, I—"

"Look," he said, "I don't want to hear no more about it. I got my mind made up."

She stared at him for a while, then said, "All right, Tony. I don't want to fight with you."

In the next few weeks Tony's life was pretty much the new routine. He slept late, then got up and saw Maria, usually, and at night went around to the houses with Leo. Often he and Leo lunched together or had a few drinks at one of the clubs, and Tony got to know the business well. He learned that the gross from the houses was about eighteen million a year, and from the half that didn't stay with the girls, Leo and Hamlin and Alterie were paid fifteen hundred a month.

After Tony had been working with Leo for about a month, he met Frank Alterie for the first time. It was a Saturday night, a busy night, and Leo was making his

fifth pickup, this one at the big house on Fillmore.
When they went in, Frank Alterie was sitting in the
parlor.

To Tony, who hadn't seen him before, he was just
another guy talking to one of the gals. But as they went
in Leo stopped suddenly and swore beneath his
breath. "I been expecting something like this," he said.

Tony glanced at him, frowning, then Leo walked
across the room and stuck out his hand, smiling pleasantly. "Hi, Frank, good to see you. Postman's holiday,
huh?" He laughed.

"Yeah."

Leo turned to Tony. Watching him closely, he said,
"Tony, this is Frank Alterie. About time you two guys
met up with each other. Frank, Tony Romero."

Alterie stood up, smiling. Tony nodded and said,
"Hello, Alterie. Glad to meet you." He stuck out his
hand.

Alterie looked at Tony's hand, then back at his face.
He was about Tony's height, but slimmer, with small
black eyes and a dark complexion. He was a sharp-
looking guy, maybe thirty, with deep waves in his slick
black hair, and dressed in a draped black suit with a
red bow tie.

"Tony Romero," he said. "Well." He smiled pleasantly. "A pleasure. A real pleasure. I hear you're
getting to be a real big pile of crap, Romero."

Tony pressed his teeth together, anger leaping into

his stomach. Alterie had made no move to shake his hand, but just as Tony was about to drop it back to his side Alterie reached forward quickly, grabbed it, and gave it a halfhearted shake and dropped it.

He rubbed his palm twice against his black coat and then said, still smiling happily, "Yes, sir, a real pleasure, Romero." He turned to Leo without pausing and added, "You two're getting thick as thieves I hear."

"We get along," Leo said dryly.

"Oh, excuse me a minute," Alterie said. He turned and took a step away, then stopped. He looked back over his shoulder at Tony and said, "You will excuse me, won't you, Romero?"

Tony knew that the other man was baiting him, trying to make him look ridiculous, foolish. He didn't answer.

Alterie walked across the room and out the door into the hall.

Leo said, "Well, what you think of him?"

"I think he's a jerk. I'll give odds he's worked himself up to this thing."

"Acts like he's got a load on. I don't mean he's plastered, either. He's in a mean mood, Tony. You want to blow and drop back later?"

Before Tony could answer, Alterie came back in and walked up to them, still smiling.

"That didn't take long," he said. "Hey, Romero, what you doing out here? I know Leo's got work to do.

You come out after a little?" He frowned. "Hey," he added, "didn't I hear you're hot for one of these beasts?"

Tony looked at Alterie without answering for a moment, then he said, "You know something, Alterie? You're a fine fellow. You seem like a real fine fellow. But your tongue don't appear attached to your brain."

Some of the others in the room had noticed that tension was building between the three men, that something seemed about to happen, and now eight or ten of the men and women were looking at them. Alterie said, "What you mean, Romero? I don't understand that. I'm just a simple guy, not no big important pile of crap." He shook his head back and forth. "I guess you're too deep for me, Romero."

Tony was coolly deliberating the question of whether he should put the slug on this guy right here in the parlor, or wait till he got him outside. Alterie started to say something else, when Maria Casino came in.

She walked across the room and spotted Tony. "Well, Tony!" she said. "I didn't know you were here."

"Hi, baby," he said.

Alterie said, "Here I am, sweetheart, rarin' to go. I been waiting for you an hour. Never saw such a popular piece." Then he stopped suddenly, as if he'd just realized something.

He looked at Tony. "Hey," he said, "Hey, now. This

cute little piece isn't the beast we were just talking about, is it? That couldn't—well, goddamn." He started to laugh.

Maria frowned and asked Tony, "What's the matter? What's so funny?"

"Nothin', honey. Unless maybe it's Alterie. He's kind of funny." Tony grinned at her.

Alterie grabbed Maria's arm and pulled her to him, slid an arm around her waist and fondled her breast. "Come on, sweetheart, I'm anxious to see what makes you so popular."

Maria glanced at Tony, frowning, but he smiled and winked, Alterie started out with her, then stopped again.

"Oh, pardon me," he said. "You gentlemen will excuse me? You'll excuse me, won't you, Romero?"

Tony knew what he was going to do now. He didn't want to raise hell in the parlor, though, unless he had to. He squinted, as if considering Alterie's request. "Well…I don't know," he said: "Ye-e-es, Frankie, you're excused."

Alterie stopped smiling, started to speak, then pulled Maria with him as he headed for the door. "Come on, sweetheart," he said, "let's have us some fun."

After they left, Leo said, "Uh, Tony, you want to blow?"

"I ought to slug him one. No sense putting it off, is

there? Go get your business done; I'll wait here in case Alterie comes out in a hurry."

Tony thought Leo looked relieved, but he also seemed to become suddenly more nervous and tense. He leaned closer and said, "He's a mean bastard, Tony. I mean it. You got to watch him."

"Go on, pick up the stuff. You can tell me how mean he is later."

Leo went out and Tony sat on the gray couch. He lit a cigarette and smoked half of it before Leo returned.

When Leo came back in he sat down by Tony and said, "We got nothin' more to do here, pal. We can take off if you're ready."

"Maybe you got nothin' more to do here. Go ahead if you want to."

"You're gonna wait for him, huh?"

"What you think?"

"O.K. I know it wouldn't look good if you took off— to Sharkey particular, but I don't like it. I tell you he's a mean bastard. He knows you're after him. He gets a chance, and you jump him, he'd like nothin' better'n a chance to kill you. Shark'd cover for him, and you'd be no more trouble to him."

Tony didn't say anything. There was a tight feeling in his stomach. He stubbed out his cigarette and lit another.

"O.K.," Leo said. "He wears a gun, just like I do. You want mine?"

Tony shook his head.

"Carries a knife, too, sometimes. You wouldn't be the first guy he used it on."

Tony inhaled deeply on the cigarette. He felt sure he could handle Alterie, but there was always a chance some damn thing could go wrong. This had to be handled now, though. Tony knew that everything that happened—and for that matter everything of any importance he'd done since he started going around with Leo—would reach Sharkey's ears in a matter of hours. And Angelo's ears.

He turned to Leo. "You sticking around?"

"Hell, yes, I am. Hell, I'm in it as much as you. I ain't gonna run out on you. Not now."

"Thanks, Leo. I knew you weren't anyway. Do one thing, will you. Don't let him pull the gun on me. I'll take care of anything else."

Leo licked his lips and nodded silently.

"Say, Leo," Tony said after a minute, "you know Alterie's district, don't you? About as well as he does?"

"Sure. Why?"

"Nothin'. I was just wondering." They waited.

Tony was beginning to feel excited. There was a muted roaring in his head that spread through his body, made him seem to tingle all over. This was a break, when you came right down to it, he thought.

He heard Alterie in the hall before he saw him. He was laughing and joking loudly with somebody, then he came through the door into the parlor. He stopped and looked at Leo and Tony.

"Well, I'll be damned," he said. "You guys still here? Hey, Romero, you waiting for me to get through, or what?" He laughed. "Worth waiting for."

He walked across the room and stopped in front of Tony and Leo as they got up from the couch. He didn't look at Leo, but he said to him, looking at Tony, "This pal of yours, he's just a kid, huh? Practically a baby. Hey, Romero, you been weaned yet?"

"Alterie, seems like you been on my back since we come in. Seems like you want some trouble with me."

Alterie dropped his voice and said softly, with no pretense of humor, "You're goddamn right, you sonofabitch. You keep your nose out of my business, or you'll get more trouble than you ever heard of. I know what you're working on, you bastard—"

Tony waved a hand, smiling pleasantly. "Wait a minute, Frank. No sense us talkin' like this. I don't want no trouble with you."

"I didn't figure you did."

"Christ, no, Frank. No reason we can't get along." Tony looked around the room, at the sober faces, then back at Alterie. "I...don't like talkin' about it in here, all these characters. Come on, let's go out to the car. We can work this out, Frank."

There was a thin, contemptuous smile on Alterie's lips. Tony threw his arm around the other's shoulders and steered him toward the hall and to the front door, saying, softly, "Christ, Frank, you don't want to get so riled up. I'm a easy guy to get along with. I never even met you before and you start right in on me. Couldn't you tell right off I didn't want no trouble with you? A couple guys can talk, can't they? Like sensible people? What got you so riled up anyway?"

They reached the front door and stepped outside. Leo came out and shut the door behind them. Tony could feel the muscles in Alterie's shoulder bunched and tight, and his head was turned to the right, looking at Tony's face, his expression unsure and thoughtful.

Tony said, "You shouldn't talk the way you did, Frank. That gets nobody nowhere." He stopped on the porch and tightened his grip on Alterie's shoulder and arm, grinning into the other face inches from his own.

Alterie frowned and started to pull away, but Tony squeezed him harder, his strong fingers biting into the other's arm just beneath the shoulder. "Sure gets *you* nowhere, Frank," he said pleasantly. Tony squeezed Alterie's arm tight and jerked the other toward him as he swung his own body to the left and whipped his right fist into Alterie's stomach. Alterie gasped and tried to lift his hand, held in Tony's grip at the bicep, and Tony released him, then swung as hard as he could into the other's stomach again. Alterie bent over, gasping and Tony planted his feet firmly and smashed his big right fist into the man's face.

Alterie staggered back against the wall of the house, arms down at his sides, and Tony stepped quickly toward him, reached under his coat and took out the gun that was there.

He tossed the automatic to Leo, then turned back to Alterie. "You had no call to talk that way," he said softly. He stepped toward Alterie just as Leo said sharply, "Watch it, watch the knife."

As Alterie lifted his hands he'd pulled from his back pocket a shiny, spring-blade knife. The six inches of steel snapped forward as Tony stopped suddenly, his eyes on the gleaming blade. Alterie held the knife down at his side, the point a few inches in front of his body weaving back and forth slowly like a snake's head. Blood trickled from the corner of Alterie's mouth; he crouched slightly, eyes on Tony's face.

When he moved, it was quick. He stepped a little to the side, then sprang forward, the keen blade ripping upward in a blurred arc toward Tony's stomach. Tony held his ground, big hands splayed out in front of him, past the knife's arc, above the man's wrist. The wrists jarred into Tony's hands as he felt the point of the knife flick at his coat and then felt the small, sharp pain over his stomach.

He clamped his fingers down on Alterie's wrist, felt his greater strength beginning to force the other man's hand back and up. He strained his muscles, lifting that hand and knife, then drove his body forward and slammed the lighter man against the wall. He twisted the arm roughly and watched Alterie's face contort with the pain, then he slowly slid his right hand down and closed it around Alterie's fist, trapping the knife there as he moved his left hand suddenly to the other's elbow. With that leverage he pulled at the elbow as he forced the firmly held hand up and back toward Alterie, the knife point bending slowly toward the man's chest.

Tony knew he had the other man now; his strength was so much greater that he could easily have broken the arm in his hands. And when Alterie tried to pull away, Tony increased the upward pressure on the elbow. Alterie wasn't looking at Tony now, but at the point of the thin knife blade as it moved an inch at a time toward him, closer, until, held in his own hand and Tony's it was touching his chest.

Tony pushed the knife forward until he felt it slide through the black coat and knew it was touching skin beneath. He said softly, grinning, tight-lipped at the other, "Easy now, Alterie. Easy. This sticker will go through you like you were butter. I oughta kill you, you sonofabitch, for talkin' to me like that."

Alterie's eyes were wide and his chin was pulled back against his chest, ripples of flesh bunched under his chin as he rolled his eyes downward to where the knife point touched his chest. His breathing was shallow through his open mouth as he strained to keep his chest away from that lethal point.

Tony looked at Alterie's face with his own eyes narrowed to bare slits and his lips pressed together. "Look at me, you sonofabitch," he said. "Now!"

Alterie, without moving any other part of his body, rolled his eyes up to Tony's. Tony grinned at him and slowly, deliberately, pressed the knife forward. Tony could feel the blade press an inch into the flesh in front of it, easily, almost as if the muscle and ligaments and fat were melting beneath the steel.

Alterie sucked in his breath suddenly, noise squeaking in his throat. His mouth was stretched wide and his lower lip danced back and forth on his teeth. His whole face began to twitch and shake as he made little squeaking, gasping noises in his throat.

Tony looked at him, feeling the knife in the man's body, and a hot flood of excitement swept over his own body, making his flesh warm. It was an almost sexual excitement, and his face was nearly as contorted as Alterie's. Tony knew that with only the slightest pressure he could thrust the knife deeper, so deep that the life under his hands would drain out slowly and Alterie would die as Tony held him impaled on the blade in his fist.

He stared into the panicked man's face and said, "I'll kill you, Alterie, I'll kill you, kill you."

Alterie's mouth twitched; tears glistened in his eyes and rolled down his cheeks. He started to sob and blubber, disgustingly, helplessly. His teeth began to chatter, the rapid clicks audible as the bones rattled together. His breath made a soft hissing noise as he sucked it through the spaces between his teeth.

Tony looked at him, his eyes cold, then he shuddered, pulled the knife from Alterie's chest and jerked it from the man's weak fingers. He threw the knife to the floor of the porch as Alterie slumped back against the wall. Tony looked at him with his lips curling, then stepped close and hit him in the stomach with all his strength. The breath spurted from Alterie's lungs like vomit as Tony caught him, held him upright with his left hand as he pumped his right fist again and again into the man's stomach and chest and face.

Alterie was unconscious before Tony hit him the last time on the mouth and felt the teeth break under his knuckles, then dropped him to the floor.

Tony turned toward Leo who hadn't said anything since he'd warned Tony about the knife. He was looking down at the crumpled form of Alterie now. "My God," he said in a whisper. "My God, Tony, you maybe killed him."

"He'll be all right, the bastard. I should have killed him for pulling that sticker on me. The bastard."

They made the last pickup on Divisadero Street, then drove to Tony's hotel. Before Tony got out he said to Leo, "Look, pal, Alterie's not gonna be up and around for a while. What happens?"

"I dunno."

"You know his district, Leo. You could take it over. Why not me take over for you until Alterie's back. I know the ropes. Then later you come back in and Alterie runs his own district again." He grinned. "If he lasts."

Leo looked at Tony strangely, then frowned. "Tony," he said slowly. "You meant it to happen like this, didn't you? You asked me in the house if I knew Alterie's district. You didn't work him over because he pulled the sticker; you had it figured then, before you even went out."

Tony didn't answer for several seconds. Then he laughed and said, "You stupid wop. What the hell give you a dumb idea like that?"

"Yeah, sure, Tony. Forget it."

Chapter Five

Almost two months after the fight, Tony was having lunch with Leo in the Domino Club. The conversation had been mostly about the houses, a few troubles, talk about Leo's women.

Then Leo said suddenly, "Well, Tony, looks like maybe you get a try."

"How you mean?"

"Alterie's spot. That's what you wanted, ain't it?"

"Christ, you mean it? This straight?"

Leo chewed on his lip. "I dunno for sure. But Shark says you're to see him tomorrow. Nine in the A.M." He shook his head. "Don't see nothing else it can be. Alterie ain't been the same since—that trouble. He's no good to Shark no more. He's on the needle good now. He's letting everything go straight to hell, too. He's out. Maybe you get in."

Tony took a deep breath and grinned tightly. "Damn," he said. "How about that. Damn, that's fine, man. Christ, I hope you're right, pal."

Tony paused in front of the tall building on Market Street, craned his neck to look up to its top. This Angelo must be some guy. He'd heard it noised around that he owned this building in which he had his office. Angelo. Louis Angelo. The Top.

The interview with Sharkey had been short and hadn't told Tony much. Sharkey had simply said that they'd been keeping an eye on him. He was to see Angelo at this address. It was almost ten in the morning, the hour when Tony was to see Angelo. He went inside.

At the tenth floor he got out of the elevator and walked down to the door lettered "National Investment Counselors," opened it and walked inside. There were chairs along the left wall and a girl sat behind a brown desk at his right. She was typing something, but looked up and smiled pleasantly when he came in.

"May I help you?"

"I'm Tony Romero. I got an appointment with Mr. Angelo."

She looked at him appraisingly for another second, then pressed a switch on a little box at the right edge of her desk, leaned forward and spoke softly into it. Then she said to Tony, "You may go in now, Mr. Romero. Through that door." She nodded toward a door in the wall.

It was a plain, heavy wooden door, with no lettering on it. Tony ran his tongue over his lips, then opened the door and walked in, shut the door behind him.

So this guy was Angelo? There was only one other

person in the room. He was a small guy sitting behind a brown desk like the one out front, and as Tony came in he leaned back in his swivel chair and looked at him. Sitting down, he looked like he couldn't be much more than five and a half feet tall, and he was a skinny egg, Tony thought. He was over forty years old, and his dark hair was graying.

Tony walked across the carpet and stopped in front of the desk. Jesus, there was something funny-looking about Angelo, he thought. The guy was thin, actually skinny, with the skin tight over his face, but he still looked flabby. That was the only way Tony could describe it to himself, as if maybe the bones inside him were flabby, like he didn't have any muscles to hold him firmly and solidly together. That was nuts, though, the guy looked like any other little skinny guy; it was just a screwy impression. Angelo's eyes were a strange pale brown, almost yellow.

He said, "You're Tony Romero?" The guy had a silky voice, soft and quiet.

"Yes, sir."

"Sit down, Tony."

Tony sat down. "I'm Angelo," the man said. He opened a desk drawer and took out a cigar, clipped off the end and stuck the cigar in his mouth. Angelo's mouth was even too small for that little face, Tony thought. Just a small, puckered ring, like rubbery lips squeezing together all the time. There was hardly room for the big black cigar. Angelo didn't look much like the Top, sitting there with that big cigar drooping out of his mouth.

Tony sat without speaking while Angelo got his cigar going and puffed on it a couple times, looking at it. Tony leaned back and crossed his legs, then Angelo said abruptly, "You're taking over Frank Alterie's district. I know everything you've done the last four months; I wouldn't be surprised if I know half the things you've thought. You'll be working for me." He looked away from his cigar for the first time and fixed the odd, yellowish eyes on Tony. "That means you never question anything I tell you, or anything Mr. Sharkey tells you for me. Understood?"

Tony hesitated only a moment, but Angelo said sharply, "Well?"

"Yes, sir. That's understood."

"Be sure it is. If it isn't, you won't work for me."

"Yes, sir. I understand. What you say goes. All the way."

Angelo puffed a couple times on his cigar. He said, "You're very fortunate, you know. You're young to be starting with me—and in Alterie's district. You were born there, weren't you, Tony?"

"Yes, sir."

"How old are you?"

"Twenty-two."

"You're a liar. Never lie to me again about anything. How old are you, Tony?"

"I'm twenty."

"You might do well, if you're a better man than Alterie. Are you?"

"Why, yes, sir."

"Because you beat him up, ruined his face? Because you're stronger than he is? Does that make you a better man than he is?"

Tony swallowed. This Angelo made him uncomfortable. He talked like a loony. Tony wondered if the guy had all his marbles.

Angelo went on without pausing, speaking softly, looking at the tip of the cigar in his small hand, "Frank Alterie forgot some of the things I told him. He forgot to conduct himself exactly as I wished. You won't do that. You'll do exactly what I wish. Right?"

"Why...sure. Yes, sir."

"I tell you to jump out the window, you jump. Right?"

Tony licked his lips. What was the bastard trying to do? The bastard was like one of them hypnotists. He got you saying yes, yes, yes, till you couldn't stop, hardly. "Yes, sir," he said.

Angelo puffed on his cigar. "Fine, Tony. Just don't forget. All right, that's all. You can go. Anything you want to ask?"

"Well...Alterie know I'm taking over?"

"No."

"You want me to start tonight?"

"Yes."

Tony stood up. "All right. And thanks very much, Mr. Angelo, for the chance."

Frank Alterie lived in the Gordon Hotel on Stockton. Tony knocked and waited as footsteps came closer, then the door was opened and Alterie stood facing him, three feet away. When he saw Tony, he frowned. That was all; he didn't speak or move. Tony walked inside, brushing past Alterie and waited till Frank shut the door and turned around.

The guy really looked sad, Tony thought. He was thinner and his skin had a pale, sickly tint. He looked almost ten years older than he had three months ago.

Alterie leaned back against the door, still not speaking, his eyes hard and full of hate, fixed on Tony. He was wearing slacks and a white shirt, and Tony could see he wasn't wearing a gun.

Finally he spoke. "Well, what you want, Romero?"

"You don't need to work tonight, Alterie. Take a vacation. From now on."

Alterie smiled slightly, lip curling alongside the red scar. "That's it, huh?"

"That's it. You're washed up."

Alterie walked away from the door and slumped in

a chair. Tony didn't take his eyes off the man. Still smiling strangely Alterie asked, "Who'd be taking over, Romero? Couldn't be you, could it?"

"Could and is. I don't figure you'll give me no trouble."

Frank shrugged and leaned his head back against the cushion behind him. "Not likely, is it?" He laughed. "I might work up nerve enough to kill you one of these days, but otherwise I won't give you no trouble." He laughed again.

Tony walked across the room and slapped the other man twice across the face. "That tongue of yours got you in a hospital sack once already. It could happen again."

Alterie didn't say anything. He pressed his palms together and squeezed his fingers around them. He looked at Tony, then looked away.

Tony said, "You got it straight, Alterie? I just had a talk with Angelo, in case you might be wondering a little. You're out. And take it from me, I don't even want to see you around. Might be a good idea for you to blow Frisco."

Alterie didn't answer, closed his eyes. Tony turned and went out. Well, that was that, he thought. By Christ, he was in now. For no good reason he didn't feel as swell about it as he'd expected to. The hell with it, it was that dumb talk with Angelo, and the screwy way Alterie had acted. Well, frig Alterie—and Angelo. Frig them all. He'd got in, got the start he'd been after. It hadn't been too tough. Sharkey, though, was going to be tougher. You couldn't just walk in and slap a guy like him around. Yeah, he'd have to spend a lot of time on the Shark.

Chapter Six

The next twelve months of Tony Romero's life went by faster than any others he had known. At first he worked harder and longer than he ever had, then the work became routine and easier. He learned that there was more to the job than just going around picking up the cash every night. He was responsible for everything in his district; any squabble that had to be solved, any trouble that came up, any pressure for extra payoffs from the beat cops or an occasional vice-squad cop, were strictly Tony Romero's responsibility.

He was making fifteen hundred dollars a month and he had a new wardrobe, a new convertible Buick sedan, and he was living in a $250-a-month flat in an apartment hotel three blocks from Sharkey's place. Maria Casino wasn't working now; she was living with Tony.

After a year Tony knew the business as well as any of the others. He knew that he'd be warned in advance of any raids—and another part of his job was to see that the houses were "respectable" when the raids came off. By now he knew all about the one-to-one-hundred chance he had of ever doing time for breaking the law, because he was now part of the world of professional

crime, and the fix was in. He knew about bonds and
habeas corpus, bribed and intimidated witnesses, bribed
police and even grafting mayors; he knew that just one
bribed juryman could cause a hung jury, and that
professional perjurers were cheap. He knew the sickening story of "justice," particularly in some local courts,
and he was already friendly with a "right" judge, who
laughed with him about the 12 ignorant "peers" who
generally sat in judgment in the jury box. He knew
about copping pleas; probation; parole; the laughable
"life" sentences even for such crimes as murder; delays
and continuances and appeals and reversals; and the
hundred other weapons in the hands of the professional
criminal.

He still occasionally saw Leo, too, although Leo
wasn't quite as friendly as he'd once been. And now
Tony figured it was time to start working on Sharkey.

There'd never be a better chance; Sharkey didn't
interfere with the three men under him, but at the
same time he never did anything to help them. He just
sat in his luxurious apartment, transmitting orders
from Angelo, and drank his bonded whiskey. He was
drinking too much of that whiskey, and Tony heard
continuing rumbles—like those he'd heard even before
he met Angelo—that Sharkey was losing favor. Anyway,
Tony had waited a year, and a year was a big slice out
of a man's life. He was ready to start.

Tony started by building up his own district, putting

into operation some of the ideas he'd had in the last year and a half. Each house already had a card file on all the girls they employed, but Tony, without consulting Angelo or anyone else, had early begun developing his own file listing name, complete description, age or approximate age, and any other intimate detail he thought would later be of benefit to him.

In a telephone conversation with Angelo he asked for and received a little more freedom in switching around the girls in his district and working on the houses. Angelo was agreeable—as long as it didn't cost him any money. Tony assured him the reverse would probably be true—and hinted, subtly, that he'd had to go ahead on his own because Sharkey…well, Sharkey didn't seem much interested. Tony got the O.K. At his own expense he hired a capable photographer who needed the money badly enough to give Tony a ridiculously low price, and he had photographs taken of all the prostitutes in his houses in two poses: in evening clothes or street clothes, and nude. Four-by-five glossy prints went into his own file, and others went into cheap albums containing pictures of the girls in each particular house.

Tony started this in only three houses at first. In two of them there hadn't been liquor. He arranged for drinks to be made available. He put in dimmer lights— blue mostly—in the parlors and rooms, bought cheap record players that played soft music. In those three

houses he instructed the girls to be more "ladylike," in
his own words: "Don't waltz up and grab the guy, see?"
Two copies of the albums were displayed in the parlor.
A man could come in, talk to the girls if he wanted to,
or be left alone while he had a highball and pored
over the album. Tony had a hunch that some of the
customers damn near got their kicks simply from the
pictures. A man could select from the photos any girl
he wanted and get her immediately if she was unoccu-
pied, in a few minutes if she was busy. Naturally this
cost a little more.

Business, instead of falling off, picked up. Tony figured it was much like buying a suit in this respect: a lot
of guys, when confronted with identical suits, one at
fifty dollars and one at a hundred, would figure the
hundred-dollar suit must be better, and pay an extra
fifty bucks for it even though it had exactly the same
texture, fit, feel and appearance.

Naturally the girls changed from one house to another and one district to another, and new girls were
coming in all the time, but at the end of a year Tony
had an active file of over a thousand girls, complete
with detailed written information and photos.

He still heard occasional rumbles about Sharkey
and from Ginny he learned Sharkey himself was nervous and worried for the first time, and now Tony
managed to see Swan again. There wasn't anything

unusual about that; Tony managed to see him every time the guy got into town. This afternoon they had a late lunch at The Blue Fox, across the street from the police station.

After their usual conversation over coffee and a highball, Tony said, "Looks kind of like Shark's goin' to pieces, huh?"

Swan lit a cigarette before answering. "What makes you say that, Tony?"

"Christ, it's no secret. He's a lush, anyway; you know that yourself."

"He likes the stuff, all right. That's what you meant?"

"Partly. But hell, Swan, you know he's no goddamn good to Angelo. He sits on his fat ass up there in the Arlington, throws a brawl once in a while. I'll bet he don't know what's goin' on ten feet from his butt. Let me ask you something, Swan. Angelo's about fed up with him, isn't he?"

Swan slowly grinned. "Tony, I see through you like you were glass. I always have."

Tony grinned back. "So O.K. I never tried to be no mystery man. But I'm right."

"Maybe, but what if you are?"

"Sharkey can't last forever. I'm the best man Angelo's got."

"Kid, you been in this racket a little over a year. There's guys been with Angelo five, ten years. Look at

Castiglio, for instance. He's had the same job under Sharkey for five years now."

"Yeah, and he's just the type to stay right where he is another fifty. He's got no ambition. No initiative. Christ, no brain! The last three months I've jumped the gross in my district ten percent."

Swan showed interest, then he frowned. "That's funny. Angelo didn't mention—" he stopped. Then he said, "How'd you manage that, kid?"

Tony told him briefly about what he'd done. Swan pursed his lips and nodded. "Good enough, Tony. You didn't do it for love of the girls, now, did you?"

"You know why I did it."

"Uh-huh."

"You can help me, Swan. You're closer to Angelo than anybody else."

Swan thought for a few seconds, then he said slowly, "I did help you once, Tony. I helped you get started. But you've only been working for Angelo a year or so. Hell, kid, you're still only—what is it, twenty-two?"

"Couple months I'll be twenty-two."

"Remember what I told you last time? About going too fast?"

"Remember what I told you then, Swan?"

"I'm still right, kid. And something else: you don't deserve anything more yet. You—"

Tony broke in almost angrily, "For Christ's sake,

Swan. Don't give me that crap. Do you deserve to be a State Senator?"

Swan flushed and Tony went on rapidly, "I don't mean nothing personal, Swan; you know that. But don't give me this crap about I don't deserve nothin' because I only been working a year or so. Crap! You know I got more on the ball than these other slobs. You might as well try to tell me the guy that's been in the Army longest oughta be Chief of Staff, or the guy's been in politics longest oughta be President, or the guy's been goin' to church longest oughta be Pope. Jesus Christ, I seen guys could make doughnuts all their life and never learn where the holes go. What the hell does how long you been doin' a thing got to do with how good you do it? Don't give me no 'seniority' bull, neither—"

Swan interrupted, waving his hand. "Whoa, kid. Don't go through the roof. I'll be damned, a speech. I don't often get to see you so wound up." Then his face sobered. "I'll tell you something, kid. Tell you why I don't think you're right for Sharkey's job yet—and that's what we're talking about." He frowned. "Tony, you're a hell of a likable kid; I've always liked seeing you around, talking to you. If I didn't, I'd kick your teeth in. Because the truth is, you're a bastard. You're a self-centered, individualistic, smart, cocky bastard. I think you'd blow up the world if you thought it'd do you some good. You'd pimp for your wife—if you had one, which I doubt you ever will—or your mother, if there was enough money in it. Look, kid. Shark and Angelo have a lot of power, whether you realize it or not; neither of them abuse it. I'm afraid you would once you got a real taste, a real feel of it."

Tony was quiet for a moment. "The hell with it," he said. He waved for more drinks. He changed the subject, but when Swan looked at his watch fifteen minutes later, as if getting ready to go, Tony said, "Say, Swan, forget that State Senator crack. Didn't mean nothin'."

"I know it."

"You know," Tony said conversationally, "I'm just now gettin' used to you bein' in the Legislature. Man, when I think of all the jobs you used to have me do when I was a kid. Didn't nobody ever try shakin' you down about that unpolitical background?"

"No. Not many know about it. You do, of course. Angelo. The gal I used to shack up with back then. A few others. Naturally my wife knows about it."

Tony shook his head. "Well, I guess you been lucky word about your old days never leaked out. Right, Senator? I imagine they got lots worse records in the legislature than yours, though."

"Uh-huh. Some would really surprise you." Swan looked at Tony, not speaking for a while, then he said, "Well, I've got to get moving. Thanks for the meal."

"Forget it. You going to see Angelo?"

"I'll see him again before I leave tomorrow."

"Well, I sure wish you'd tell him what a great guy I am. But, I guess you know what you're doin', Swan." He grinned as they got up from the table.

Swan said quietly, "I'll think about it. You're positive your business has picked up quite a bit?"

"Sure I am. Why?"

"Nothing." They walked to the front of the restaurant. As they separated to go in opposite directions Swan shook Tony's hand and said, "Sometimes I wish I didn't understand you so well."

"Huh? What's that mean?"

"Nothing much. I just wish I didn't know how big a bastard you really are. Well, see you, kid."

"So long, Swan."

The next day Tony went to Leo's apartment in the Strand and spent an hour with him. The last half hour of conversation was the important part from Tony's viewpoint.

He started it by saying, "There's a noise that Sharkey's about out, Leo. That should make you happy."

"What you mean?"

"Well, if the Shark goes out, who goes in? Somebody has to take over Shark's spot. You're the only man in sight."

Leo got out a cigarette and tapped it against his thumbnail. "You think so?"

"Christ, there's only you and Hamlin left that got important spots—besides me. You been under Shark for five years now. Two more than Hamlin. Who you think would take over?"

"I hadn't thought a hell of a lot about it." Leo's thin face brightened a little. "Wonder how much Shark drags down."

"I dunno. But I'll bet he makes close to half-million a year."

Leo whistled, blinked his dark eyes rapidly. "That's a pile. I tried to figure it a few times; he must drag down a helluva mess."

"Yeah." Tony frowned. "But the way it's goin', Shark might last for years—unless somebody needles that Angelo. Hell, he's so far up in that office building of his, he don't know what goes on down here. He probably don't know how close Shark is to goin' clear off his nut."

"Maybe."

"Maybe, hell. Who's told him? Shark? Somebody oughta put a bug in Angelo's ear—in the interest of the business. I imagine Angelo would like to know it; oughta appreciate getting the lowdown." He paused. "Maybe I'll give him a ring myself."

"You think he ought to be told, huh?"

"What do you think, Leo? Put yourself in Angelo's spot. Wouldn't you appreciate a little tip that the number-one guy under you was about off his rocker, drinking like a fish, maybe—maybe even gettin' his accounts messed up a little?" He shrugged. "Hell, Angelo probably got a fair idea, but no real lowdown."

"What you mean about accounts?"

"Just a stab in the dark. Funny thing. I saw Swan yesterday and mentioned business picked up in my district—you know, one of those periodic up-and-down swings—and it seemed to surprise Swan. I guess Angelo didn't know nothin' about it. I don't figure it. I don't suppose Shark would hold out on the Top."

"No," Leo said. "Don't seem likely."

They chatted for a few more minutes, then Tony got up. "Guess I'll blow. Take a sleep before I start around tonight."

Leo took him to the door. "You think you'll put a bug in Angelo's ear?"

"I dunno. I don't know him too good—you know him better'n I do. Probably wouldn't hurt none. Well, I gotta beat it, Leo. How about lunch tomorrow?"

"O.K. One at the Domino O.K.?"

"See you at one, Leo."

Angelo looked up. "Hello, Tony. Sit down."

Tony sat down in a chair at the end of the desk. This was the fourth time he'd been up here; once when Angelo told him he was taking over Alterie's spot— fourteen months ago now—then a couple of times in the next six months on business matters that Angelo wanted to talk to Tony about. One of those times a "reform" administration had come in, and things were tough for a couple months until Angelo finally met the D.A.'s price. But this was the first time Tony had been here for several months.

Angelo blinked his yellowish eyes and looked at Tony. "My reports, and the ones you've sent me, show your district is doing quite well, Tony. I remember our phone conversation about a few changes you wished to make, but I'd like you to tell me exactly what you've done."

Angelo got out a black cigar and lighted it, then stuck it into his puckered mouth. Tony was thinking that Angelo knew damn well everything he'd done, but he started talking anyway.

"In the last four months the gross from my district has gone up fifteen and a half percent." Tony had hired an accountant for two days, given him a pile of figures, and learned about his own business in terms of percentages. He went on, "The organization's net for the district went up fourteen and two tenths percent in the same period—I had to spend a little money. Part of the reason for the net being almost as much as the gross is that we didn't have to pay any more protection. Maybe that'll change, I don't know about that. Also—"

Angelo interrupted. "Have you any idea what's happened in the other two districts in the same period?"

Tony almost smiled. He'd been nervous about this conversation, but he'd planned what he'd say. "Yes, sir. Leo's went down four percent, Hamlin's three."

"Then part of your increase was from the other areas."

"Yes, sir. But only a small part. Less than half, because my district's the biggest grosser; always was. Except for the phone stuff."

Angelo didn't say anything. He sat quietly behind his desk. The quiet lasted so long that finally Tony said, "Mr. Angelo, those three houses I mentioned, those were the only ones I made specials. Before I went any farther, I figured I'd better ask what you thought about it. There's several other things I'd like to do, too, if you figure it's O.K."

"What things, Tony?"

"One thing, it seems like we don't have no special house for the nutty characters. Some of these guys go to the regular places—but we're not really set up for that. I was thinking maybe a special house, just set aside for them guys, might make a hundred thousand a year, maybe a quarter million."

He stopped, wondering what Angelo would say. Angelo took the cigar from his mouth and stared at it. "You've given this quite a bit of thought, I take it."

"Yes, sir. I got a file on most of the girls, and I know just the ones would be perfect for a place like that. I even looked over a place out on Army Street you could probably get real cheap." Tony swallowed. This was the first time he'd ever mentioned to anybody that he was keeping a file on the prostitutes. He hoped to Christ Angelo would ask him about it now that it had slipped, apparently casually, into the conversation. If not, he'd have to mention it again himself.

But Angelo looked at Tony. "What file is this? What kind of file?"

"I got a file on about twelve hundred girls we got now, or worked for us. Card file with almost everything about them—what kind of tricks they turn, looks, how much they make and so on. And the pictures like in them three houses I mentioned."

Angelo frowned. "Why didn't I know about this, Mr. Romero?"

Tony said pleasantly, "Well, it was just something I worked up. I liked to figure what girls was doin' best, what kind of play they get. It was more for my own personal use than anything else—so I could see the girls got in the right spots, and so on. I figured it wouldn't do no harm. Besides, this last year I had some extra time on my hands."

"You don't have nearly that many girls in your district, Mr. Romero."

Tony wished the guy would stop calling him Mr. Romero. Usually Angelo wasn't so formal. Maybe he'd put his foot in it. Well, the hell with it; a guy had to take a chance if he was ever going to get anywhere. He said, "No, sir. That includes girls in all the districts, all over San Francisco. But that's because we shift the girls from one place to another. Every time girls would come into my spots I'd add 'em to my file." He hesitated, then added, "I never went outside my district for none of it; it was just when they was shifted."

"I see," Angelo said.

Nothing was said for what Tony figured was at least five minutes. It seemed to him like an hour. Then Angelo rolled the ash off his cigar and said, "I like to see a man with initiative, Tony, and one who is willing to work. However, in the future, I think you'd better advise me quite closely of your plans." He paused. "You may go ahead with that special location you described. Just go ahead with the rest in your own way—but keep me informed."

"That's swell, Mr. Angelo. Thanks."

"Do you carry a gun?"

"Why, no, sir." Tony never had worn a gun since he'd started. For one thing, he had seen too many guys in trouble because they'd carried a heater, and used it. And the "wrong" cops were always giving a gun-toter more trouble than guys who were clean. Besides, Tony had plenty of confidence in his fists and strength if there was ever any trouble.

Angelo said, "That's all, Tony. I suppose you have work you want to do."

"Yes, sir. I'm anxious to get started."

Tony started for the door but Angelo stopped him. "I think you'd better buy a gun, Tony. Get it this afternoon. Franzen's Sporting Goods carries what you'll want. Incidentally, you will have no trouble getting a gun permit. I'd suggest you take care of that this afternoon, also."

Tony felt exhilaration leaping inside him. Angelo wouldn't have told him to carry a gun unless he had bigger things planned for him. Or maybe he just didn't want to take a chance on Tony getting robbed some night. No telling. Tony said, "Fine, Mr. Angelo. I'll take care of it." He went out.

He headed down Market Street. It was already two in the afternoon. He had to arrange for the gun permit, then drop in at Franzen's and pick up a gun. Christ, he didn't even know how to use a gun, not enough to hit anything with one. He guessed he'd have to learn. Funny Angelo's suddenly bringing that up. You couldn't really figure the guy. It was funny, though.

Chapter Seven

It was Saturday night, a week after Tony's talk with Angelo. In the bedroom of his apartment he put on a clean white shirt, then slipped gold links into the French cuffs. He selected a maroon foulard from the three dozen ties on the rack and tied it in a wide knot, then put on the coat to the chocolate-brown suit. He looked pretty good, he thought.

Maria called from the living room, "Tony, honey, you goin' out again tonight?"

"Yeah, honey. Business."

"I thought maybe we'd go out. We haven't been out on a Saturday night for months. Can't we, Tony?"

He said, "Remember I told you about talking to Angelo last week?"

"Uh-huh."

"Well," he grinned at her, "it looks like maybe I get Sharkey's spot. I didn't want to mention it till I was pretty sure, but it looks good. How does that sound, baby?"

She sighed. "All right, I guess."

"You *guess?* What you mean, you guess? Christ, I thought you'd be tickled pink. If I get in we'll have so much dough we'll be throwin' it out the window."

"Tony." She reached for his hand and held it. "I know you don't like for me to talk about it, but...I wish you weren't gettin' in so deep. You're makin' plenty money now, but you keep on the way you're going, one of these days you won't never be able to get out."

"Get *out?* What in hell's got into you? Who wants out? I'm gonna be somebody, baby. This is just the start for me—for us. Hell, this is what I really been waitin' for."

"Tony, you think you know everything—you don't even know what this business is really like. It's mean and filthy and cruel."

"I suppose you know more than I do about it, huh?" His voice was sharp, angry.

"Some of it—now, don't get mad, Tony. But don't forget I was working in the houses a year before you even thought about it. I was right down on the bottom, and you get a different picture of it from there. Honey, you sit up on top of it all, look down to the houses like they were part of a machine. You're just workin' yourself into the middle. There's a lot of people under you, and Angelo on the other side— and a lot more over him. In the long run you'll just get yourself in trouble, maybe get yourself kicked out or killed or something awful. Look at Alterie—and now maybe Sharkey."

"You're a sweet one, you are. I tell you something I

think you'll be real happy about and you start giving me a goddamn beef. Jesus, don't you want me never to get noplace?"

She chewed on her plump lower lip. "I'm sorry, Tony. Forget it, huh? But you've—already you've changed. You're not like you were."

"Who the hell wants to be like I was? I should wear a diaper all my life?" He stood up.

Maria pressed her lips together, then suddenly changed the subject. "Gee, you look nice, Tony. Real sharp in that new suit."

He glanced down at it. "Not bad, huh—oh, hell."

He went into the bedroom and took a heavy .45 automatic and leather shoulder harness from the dresser, shrugged out of his coat and strapped on the gun and holster, then put the coat on over it. The gun made a bulge at his left armpit. Too goddamn big. He should have got one of them dinky guns that wouldn't bulge so much. But he figured he'd better wear the thing tonight. Angelo had told him to get it, and these were Angelo's boys he was seeing. He glanced at the new watch on his wrist, diamonds replacing the numerals. They'd be here in about ten minutes.

"What they going to do with you?" Maria sounded worried.

"I dunno." Swan hadn't known either. He thought about that talk with Swan, frowning. That had been a nutty deal. The guy phoned him, told him there'd be some of Angelo's boys checking up on him, maybe taking him out on the town. It would seem casual, an accidental meeting, but Angelo had set it up to get a close check on the way Tony handled himself. Tony had started to thank Swan volubly, but Swan had interrupted him.

"Listen, Tony. I'm sticking my neck out to tell you this, and I don't want you to labor under the delusion you blackmailed me into doing it."

"You lose your marbles? What you talkin' about?"

"I'm out of knee-pants, kid. I didn't miss the point when you were talking about my 'unpolitical background' the other day over lunch. I wouldn't put it past you. But that's not my reason."

"Ah, Swan. Don't talk like that. That's a crazy way to talk."

Swan didn't answer. Finally Tony asked, "Shark's out for sure, huh?"

"That's right, Tony. In his job he knows too much; he knows who gets paid off and how much, which cops and judges and officials are right and which are wrong, a hundred things like those that whoever takes over from him will have to know, too. And when you know that much, Tony, you've got to be damned careful. Shark drinks too much and sometimes talks too much drunk. And—" he hesitated—"there's a good chance he's been holding out some of the take on Angelo. Things to remember, kid."

"Well, thanks for tellin' me, Swan. I sure appreciate it."

"Don't thank me. I don't have any thanks coming. Tony, this is the last payment of any and all debts, past, present, and future. This is the last time I'll help you, or even think about helping you. You might even call it the coup de grace."

"What the hell you talkin' about?"

"From here to—to wherever you wind up, you're on your own. At least as far as I'm concerned. So long, kid."

"So long, Swan. And thanks, I mean it—"

"I told you, goddammit, don't thank me." He hung up.

Tony looked at the phone, then hung up the receiver. It had sounded like Swan was brushing Tony off this time. Well, the hell with Swan; he didn't need him—or anybody else.

The chimes rang in the apartment and Tony blinked, then went to the door and opened it. He liked those chimes; they had a classy sound. Two men stood outside the door. "Hi," Tony said. "Come on in."

The men came in, removing their hats and light topcoats. The meeting with them had been "accidental" enough. Tony had been having lunch with Leo when they'd showed up and Leo had invited them to the table. They'd been very friendly with Tony and the four of them had lunch. That had been two days ago and the date had been made for the three of them to go out tonight. They'd claimed to be in the same business in Chicago, out here till a Congressional investigation blew over. Some Senators were putting on a big show to impress their constituents; elections weren't far off.

"How about a drink?" Tony asked them.

They nodded and said it might chase the fog out of their stomachs. Joyce was the big one, a guy about two hundred pounds, whose name didn't fit him. He was a tough, solid-looking man with a pouchy, expressionless face and huge gray eyes that looked almost white against his dark skin. The other one was tall, slim and wiry as a whip, with a long, hooked nose and decaying teeth. He was called Frame. Tony didn't know whether that was an underworld moniker, or the guy's real name. Tony didn't ask. Frame wasn't the kind of guy you asked personal questions, even though he was always kidding around and cracking wise.

Tony asked what they wanted, then had Maria get busy at the small portable bar in the corner while he showed Joyce and Frame around the apartment. He was proud of the place: the big living room with a wide window toward the bay, even though only a small slice of the bay could be seen past other apartment houses; the heavy maroon drapes at the side of the window, drapes that could be opened or closed by pulling, with only two fingers, the cord at the side of the window;

the bedroom with its twin beds, the black-and-white-tiled bathroom, modern kitchen and extra sitting room, all of it furnished in modern style.

Tony introduced the two to Maria, introducing her as his wife; then they finished their drinks and took off. He had promised to show them around his district, so they started for there in Tony's Buick sedan, with the top up. It was a cold night, the fog thick and swirling.

Chapter Eight

Tony felt sick. He didn't think he could make it. It was Sunday night, and he was still feeling the effects of the drinking bout. He didn't even remember going to bed after leaving Joyce and Frame at the Leopard Room. Jesus, that had hit him all of a sudden. Those guys must be in good shape, he thought, calling him again, telling him to come on up to this poker game.

Tony checked the address. This was it. The game was in room 16. He started up. They must know enough about him now, he thought; what the hell was a poker game for? He had a funny feeling about it, but maybe that was because he still had a hangover. Frame, who had phoned him, had said it was just a friendly, private little game. Tony smiled to himself thinking that at least Frame hadn't sounded very cheerful; he probably felt worse than Tony.

Christ, this was a dump. Hell of a neighborhood, too. Tony shifted the big .45 under his coat. He wore it all the time when he was around Joyce and Frame, and in this kind of neighborhood a guy might need it. Beat-up shacks and dumpy hotels, mangy dogs and mangier winos. The place gave him the creeps.

He found room 16 on the second floor and knocked.

Joyce opened the door, blinked his gray eyes at Tony. He grunted, "Come on in, Romero. I hope you don't hold onto your money like you hold bourbon."

Tony grinned at him and walked into the room then stopped suddenly, feeling his heart kick in his chest, and his skin get cold.

He looked at the man sitting at the far end of the table, finally found his tongue. "Well, hi," he said. "Hi, Sharkey."

Sharkey looked up and said pleasantly, "Hello, Romero. What you doin' here? Didn't know you were a poker player."

Tony swallowed and looked around. He saw Frame and Joyce, and two other guys he didn't know. This didn't look good at all. He said, "Yeah, I'm a poker man from way back, Shark." He nodded at the others, then grinned at Frame.

"How you feel, Frame? Like a shot?"

"You bastard." He grinned, showing the darkened, pitted teeth. "I shouldn't never drink with you again."

Tony said, "You know, after I left you guys I really got high."

"You didn't have no more, did you?"

"No, it just caught up with me."

The others sat down around the green-felt covered table—a regular poker table, Tony noted. Maybe they had a lot of games up here. He sat down at the one empty chair, Joyce on his left and Frame on his right,

Sharkey across from him flanked by the two other men. Tony was introduced to the others. Pudge was the short, fat one; Marzo was the stupid-looking guy with the big chin and the long, slim fingers. A thought came to Tony: maybe the game was rigged, maybe they'd thrown a pro in to deal and plant Tony with good hands or bad ones. What for? Take him for his dough? See if he'd know he was being cheated? Maybe let him know the game was rigged and see how he'd handle himself? But what was Shark doing here if it was one of those things? He glanced at Shark, then around the table. There wasn't much talk or joking yet, the way a lot of games were. Tony played a good deal of poker, but usually they were friendly games, not the quiet, soft-voiced games the pros often played. He liked a little life and conversation.

Joyce broke out a new deck, tossed the jokers aside and slipped the cards into the middle of the table, shuffled them, passed them on. They cut for deal, with Marzo cutting a king high, then Joyce got up and went to the corner of the room where a table was set up with bottles and glasses on it. He mixed six drinks and brought them back. He gave Tony the first one.

"Here," he said. "Unless you got no stomach at all, this should feel good after last night."

Tony started to shake his head, then took the drink. A drink would taste good, at that. He could beg off after one or two, and he didn't want to antagonize anybody yet, not till he knew what the score was. Maybe the score was just a poker game for the hell of it. But there was something in the air....

Joyce said, "Table stakes?" They all nodded and he went on, "Ante five, check stud cinches, dealer's choice but no goddamn whorehouse games. Play poker, right?"

That suited everybody. Tony thought this might wind up a cutthroat game. The men stacked their money in front of them as Marzo shuffled the cards expertly, slapped them down for Joyce to cut, then tossed them around the table, dealing to the next man before the first card hit the table. The guy really handled the pasteboards. Marzo had a thick pile of green bills in front of him, weighted with a silver dollar. Tony had about $1400 on the table. Marzo was dealing draw, jacks or better. Tony picked up his five cards and bunched them, then spread them slowly. A pair of tens. Pudge opened for twenty bucks; Tony called, thinking he'd ride along a while till he saw how the game went. He had a swallow of his drink.

Only Joyce and the dealer threw in their cards. The opener drew three cards; Frame drew two cards to Tony's three; Sharkey drew one. Pudge bet thirty bucks. Frame called. Tony had drawn a pair of sixes to go with his tens; he called. Sharkey raised thirty, Pudge dropped out, and Frame called. Frame had drawn two, Sharkey one. That one-card draw might mean two pairs—but Frame had called. Tony folded.

Sharkey won the pot with a small straight. Christ, Tony thought, a straight on the first hand; Shark would have won three or four times as much if he'd got that hand five minutes later when the game loosened up. Frame lost with aces over nines; Tony made a mental note that Frame had drawn to a pair, holding an ace kicker. And that dumb Pudge bet pairs into one-card draws. Jesus. This could cost a guy plenty.

Frame dealt draw again. Tony swallowed half his drink before he picked up his hand, maybe he could drown the butterflies in his stomach. Tony had nothing and threw in his hand when the pot was opened. This was a hell of a game. Everybody sat around quietly, concentrating on their cards. It was too goddamn quiet. All that was said was the amount of the bet, and "call," or "raise," or "check." He wondered again what Sharkey was doing here. And those two guys, Pudge and Marzo. Come to think of it, Tony hadn't ever been around Sharkey except up at the Shark's apartment. Tony felt uneasy; he looked across the table at Shark. The man looked nervous and ill at ease, himself. Sharkey caught Tony's eye and stared at him for several dragging seconds, then looked at his hand, threw it into the middle of the table. He licked his red lips, got up and walked toward the open door leading into the adjoining bathroom.

Maybe, thought Tony, he was imagining it, but it seemed that all the others present stopped moving for a half second and looked at Sharkey. Frame said, "I'm done," shoved back his chair as he threw in his cards, then got up and followed Sharkey into the john. The hand ended and Tony shuffled for his deal. Christ, he was nervous; seemed like he was all thumbs. He slapped the cards down for the cut and his palm brushed the top of the pack as he took his hand away, cards fanning on the table. Pudge stacked them, cut, shoved the deck to Tony. While he dealt, Shark and Frame came back and sat down. Nobody said anything. Tony could feel his muscles tense, pulling in his arms as he dealt. This was no good; this was the crap. There was something he didn't know about. Tony picked up his hand and looked at Sharkey. The guy didn't look good at all; his face was pale, perspiration gleaming on his high forehead. Sharkey looked around the table, let his glance stop on Tony, swallowed, tried to smile, red lips twisting. He looked funny. Everything looked a little funny.

Tony examined his cards as the man on his left opened. Pair of threes. He started to throw his hand in, then saw that he had four spades. One of the threes was a spade. What was the matter with him? He'd damn near thrown away a four card flush. He reached for the money in front of him. "Call. Uh, what's the bet?"

"Fifty."

He tossed two twenties and a ten into the pot.

He dealt himself a diamond. Crap. What lousy luck. Must be half a G in the pot now. He dropped out. Sharkey won the hand. Joyce riffled the cards, put them in front of him, then got to his feet.

"Drink up," he said. "Let's loosen up. Party's too damn dead." He waited with his fists on his hips. Tony swallowed the last of his drink. The others finished theirs and Joyce quickly made more and brought them back.

He dealt. Tony squeezed his hand open. Seemed like the cards wanted to stick together; they were thick, too thick. Ace of clubs. Four, five, six, seven of hearts. Straight heart flush. This had to be it; he hadn't won a hand yet. Must be out a couple hundred. The pot was opened and Tony raised when the bet reached him. He couldn't remember the original bet. He pulled a hundred-dollar bill from the bottom of his stack and shoved it forward. "Raise."

"Cards?"

Up to me. What've I got? Get rid of that damn ace, that black bullet. "One card," he said. Gimme the eight of hearts, he thought. Gimme the heart three. The card fell in front of him. Christ, it was a long way off. He looked up. Everybody was way off, clear the hell over there around the table. He felt light. His head felt like cotton. He thought of his head floating up toward the ceiling and his neck stretching after it like a string on a balloon. He laughed at the thought.

He saw Sharkey looming closer, his heavy face suddenly growing larger in Tony's eyes. Sharkey's red lips, those stupid damn lips, were moving, but he wasn't saying anything, just mumbling. What was he saying? He looked scared.

Suddenly Tony felt panicky, a slow, erratic pulse ticking, the blood squirting from his heart and slapping against the hollow of his throat. He looked around. Everybody was staring at him, Sharkey's white face seeming closest, lips still moving. Tony needed a drink; he reached for the glass and saw it tip slowly as if somebody were pulling it by an invisible cord. It fell soundlessly to the green felt and the liquor spread in a dark stain. Tony saw the stain cover the card before him; he fumbled for the card, picked it up and put it with the others in his hand. He felt sick, dizzy, his head was floating. He was moving around the table, they were all moving, the table was spinning, spinning slowly in a tight circle, gathering speed, the frozen faces all around him blurring, melting, congealing.

Tony gasped and shook his head, squeezing his eyes together. He opened his eyes and stared; for a moment everything was clear and he saw Sharkey start to get up, saw Marzo reach out with his long, delicate-fingered hand and grasp Sharkey's shoulder, saw Sharkey look around him, his lips moving and twisting as he sank back into his chair. Tony tried to get up but his legs wouldn't push him up; it was as if his legs weren't there. The table started spinning again, faster and faster until everything was a blur and there were no faces, nothing except confused color, which deepened, became darker, and then was black, a soundless black, soft, quiet, deeper than night.

Blackness became grayness, then a pinkish glow beyond his eyelids. He forced them open as something shook him roughly. A man's face was close to his own, short stiff whiskers poking from the chin. Tony hadn't seen him before. The man moved away and Tony tried to sit up, got to one elbow. He was on a couch, and he pulled himself around till his back was against the cushions, the exertion increasing a knifing pain in his skull.

He could see the man now. A policeman. A uniformed policeman whom Tony didn't recognize. Tony shut his eyes again and put his hand against his forehead. It felt icy cold and hard to the touch. Once as a kid Tony had been delirious, sick, dreaming while awake that he was running on the tiny earth as it spun beneath his feet while all the others of the world chased him for something he had done; he had cried out in the night and nobody answered and he was afraid. His head, then, had felt this way, cold and damp and hard, and now he felt again the same fear in his mind and body.

Someone struck him across the cheek, whipping his

head around with pain roaring inside it. He opened his eyes and looked at the policeman standing over him. He looked past the man, around the room. Everybody else was there. What had happened? He'd passed out, got sick and blanked out. He saw long wiry Frame, pouchy-faced Joyce with the blank gray eyes blinking at him, Pudge, Marzo. There'd been somebody else. Sharkey. Where was the Shark?

Tony looked to his right and saw him. The poker table had been moved, and he could see Shark lying face down on the floor, oddly crumpled, the back of his head gone. Tony stared at him, uncomprehending for one moment, his mind dazed and sluggish. He realized after a while that Shark must have been shot in the forehead, the bullet ripping away the back of his skull as it smashed through. Tony raised his eyes to the wall. There was a bullet hole there, surrounded with the stain of red and ugly spots of...his stomach churned and a vile wetness rose in his throat.

He heard the cop talking to him, asking him why he'd killed Sharkey, saying they were taking him to headquarters. There was another cop in the room. He was plainclothes, but Tony figured he had to be a cop; he was a new one and he worked with the uniform. They both tore after Tony with harsh words. The uniform cop slammed his fist into Tony's face and Tony barely managed to turn enough so that the blow struck his chin and cheek instead of the middle of his mouth.

The blackness surged closer again, and he felt his lips puffing.

Then Frame was saying, "He just went off his nut, see? We were playin' poker and the guy was drinkin' heavy. All of a sudden he goes off his rocker and yells at Sharkey 'Get away from me—don't let him get me.' Then he yanks out the barker and bangs him. Smack in the biscuit. Then Romero flopped down on the floor, cold. I guess the sight of poor Sharkey's think-pot flying through the air like that put him under a strain." Frame grinned wolfishly, his stained, pitted teeth jutting under his pulled back lip.

"Come on, Romero. Lets go." It was the harness-cop speaking.

"Listen, you're crazy. I didn't drop nobody. I got nothin' to do with this." Tony's words were thick and slurred.

The cop chuckled. "You lousy crum."

Tony reached under his coat, felt the empty harness. He'd known the gun would be gone. The cop grabbed his arms and pulled him to his feet. He stood, swaying slightly, his legs weak beneath him. Then, suddenly, Angelo was in the room. Tony hadn't heard him knock, hadn't even seen him come in, but the door was open and Angelo was standing inside the room.

Angelo looked around, his face stern, the yellowish eyes hard and cold in his thin face. He spotted Joyce and said, "Thanks for calling me. What's the rest of it?" He gave Sharkey only a glance, then listened to Joyce explaining about the trouble. Angelo walked over before Tony and said in his silken voice, "You stupid fool. You idiot!" He drew back his hand and slashed it across Tony's face, glared at him a moment, then turned and walked over to the officers.

Tony followed him with his eyes, lips pressed together and his eyes squinting, almost shut. Anger boiled in him. Someday this bastard Angelo would get paid back for that.

Angelo spoke in low tones to the officers, then the three of them walked to the poker table, now in the corner of the room. Tony could see the mound of bills, apparently left there after the shooting. Angelo piled the bills in the center of the table, then rapidly leafed through them, as if counting.

Tony was still dizzy, his legs and stomach weak. He sank back down onto the couch, sat there breathing through his mouth, wondering if he'd be sick. Minutes passed, then he heard the door open. He looked up to see the coppers leaving, shutting the door behind them.

Angelo said, "Get up, Romero."

Tony got to his feet.

Angelo looked around. "Frame," he said. "You get this sonofabitch home. Joyce, you come with me."

Tony didn't understand any of it yet; his mind was still sluggish, frozen. Frame came over to him and took his arm, pulled him to his feet. Joyce and Angelo went out and Frame and Tony followed, leaving Pudge and Marzo with Sharkey's lifeless body. As Tony went out, he glanced at the poker table. The green felt was bare. There was no longer any money on it.

Frame drove Tony's Buick and left him at the apartment. Nothing was said. Tony sat in the living room while Maria made black coffee for him. Her face was drawn and worried, but she didn't try to question him after he told her to shut up and let him think.

After black coffee and a hot and cold shower, Tony lay awake in bed long after the lights were out, not speaking, but feeling Maria move restlessly at his side. He went back over it all, his mind clearer. It looked very much as if Angelo had bought off the cops; nothing new in that, it happened every day. But Tony knew now it was more than that. Angelo had merely paid them for acting out a part; that, and to button their lips about a little murder. Tony knew he hadn't killed Sharkey. He'd obviously been drugged, then somebody—one of the men present—had taken Tony's gun and shot the Shark in the forehead. Tony had no doubt at all that the officers had been the McCoy— and they had his gun. The gun he'd bought himself, had a permit issued for, and which ballistics could show was the murder gun. That was enough even without the four "witnesses" to the murder.

Tony Romero, fall guy. It was neat, though, he had

to admit it. He thought about Angelo, about Angelo's cursing and slapping him, and even while he hated him he grudgingly admitted to himself that you had to hand it to the little bastard, had to give him credit. Sharkey was out for good—and the kill was beautifully tailored for Tony. Actually, Tony wasn't much upset about that part of it. He had to admire Angelo for the way he'd handled it.

But Tony Romero was Angelo's man now; Angelo had him, had him good. The old, unsolved murder of Al Sharkey might suddenly be solved if Tony should get out of line.

He rolled over on his side and went to sleep.

Chapter Nine

Interview number five with Louis Angelo. This was the biggest one yet, thought Tony. Last night Sharkey had suddenly ceased being number-one man under the Top. This afternoon…well, Tony would see. Nothing had yet been said by either Angelo or himself since he came in and Angelo had nodded him to his usual chair.

Angelo was getting his cigar lighted. Tony watched him, waited for him to start the ball rolling. This interview might go a little differently, thought Tony. For two very dissimilar reasons: first, he actually respected Angelo more; and second, he hated him more. And Tony figured he'd been kissing Angelo's behind in these interviews long enough.

Finally Angelo said, "I knew, of course, that you wanted Sharkey's job badly; I didn't think, however, you wanted it badly enough to kill him."

"As usual, you were right. I wanted it, but not enough to knock him off."

"You did kill him, however. Isn't that right, Tony?"

"Yes, sir. I imagine the gun I did it with is down at the station now."

Angelo favored Tony with one of his rare smiles. He didn't look quite as frozen and bony when he smiled.

Maybe the change in the shape of his mouth had something to do with it. That round-eye mouth.

Angelo said, "That's right, Tony. The men who took your automatic with them were Sergeants Ellis and Cowen. Ellis, oddly enough, is with the vice squad. He just happened to be with Cowen of Homicide."

Tony didn't say anything.

"Why did you do it, Tony? How did you feel when you shot him?"

Tony said, sober faced, "Well, Mr. Angelo, it's hard to say. I never shot anybody before. I guess you'd say I felt…well, dopey. And then I got all excited when I shot him, all churned up inside. I got so excited I passed out."

Angelo smiled faintly. Tony got out a cigarette and lit it. They understood each other. Tony spent another half hour in the office, and the conversation became more businesslike, concerned with broad and specific details of running the houses. Sharkey was out now, and his killer, Tony Romero was in. It was that simple, thought Tony; or that complicated.

Just before Tony left Angelo said, "You remember our first conversation, Tony?"

"I remember it."

"Don't ever forget it. Don't ever forget, either, that you killed Sharkey, or why he was killed, or that he *is* dead."

"I got a good memory."

"Fine. One other thing, Tony. Perhaps you should inform Mrs. Sharkey of the reason for her husband's, ah, continued absence."

Ginny? Christ, didn't she know yet? "Sure," Tony said. "I'll tell her." He paused. "Well, I'll get to work on the queer house and the movies and stags, all the rest of it. O.K. to go ahead, huh?"

"Yes. Keep in mind, Tony, that I have a number of other interests besides your, ah, end of it. You have carte blanche as long as you keep me completely informed." He sighed and shook his head. "That was one of the late Mr. Sharkey's troubles: he failed to keep me informed."

Tony nodded and went out. What the hell was cart blawnsh?

Ginny let him in. She didn't look like she'd been bawling. "Hello, Ginny."

"Well, Tony! You haven't been around for almost a month. Want a drink?"

"Well, I could use one. Uh, I came to tell you something about Sharkey. About Al."

"May his dear slobbish soul rest in peace," she said. "Scotch and water?"

"Yeah. You know he got pushed?"

"I knew it about an hour after it happened. They got you tagged for it, haven't they?"

"Yeah. I didn't push him, though."

"I didn't think you did. You're not the type." She peered at him. "Not yet, you're not." She started mixing the drinks.

Tony watched her, somewhat puzzled. "Well, Ginny, I see you're all broke up over this calamity. Don't go to pieces."

She glanced up and smiled. "Don't cry for me, Tony, honey. I feel as broken up as if I'd just heard somebody chipped a piece off the rock of Gibraltar. And speaking of chipping off a piece..." She finished the drinks and brought one to him. "I haven't seen you for a hell of a time."

Tony shook his head. "Poor Sharkey."

"He wasn't so poor. I made damn sure he fixed up a will with my name plastered all over it. He had maybe three million. It's mine now, honey. And you know something? He didn't rent this apartment; he bought it. His for life." She looked around, a smug, pleased smile on her face. "The apartment's mine now, too."

That was hell. Tony had been kind of hoping he could get the place. It was a nice apartment.

"Yes," Ginny said. "I'm a rich widow, Tony. I'm a rich, horny widow."

Tony shook his head again and started to sit down in an overstuffed chair. She caught his arm. "Not that little chair, honey. That big leather one. That one over there, Tony, honey, honey."

*

Tony started working in earnest the next day. He bought a new gun and holster, a smaller gun this time: a .357 Magnum with a 3½ inch barrel, and had suits made and so tailored that the bulge wouldn't show. He made an appointment, through contacts he now had, with a dealer in pornography; he saw Leo Castiglio and told him how sorry he was that Leo hadn't been shoved into Shark's spot, but—well, he guessed Angelo knew what he was doing.

He put one of the men under him to work getting a list of all the conventions due in or near San Francisco. He got his photographer to take pictures of any prostitutes not already in his file, and brought his file completely up to date. He went carefully through that file, selecting certain cards and photos and clipping them together in special groups.

Tony drove around Frisco in his Buick, casing locations for a couple houses he wanted to start. He found many that suited his purpose, even finding a closed-down nightclub that might be turned to good purpose some day in the future. A guy could put a few wheels in it, if the place were fixed up a bit, some girls dressed in evening gowns to mix with the guys as they made their bets, and to take the chumps upstairs after they'd lost enough dough.

Tony had looked up *carte blanche* in a dictionary.

Chapter Ten

After a month, what Tony called the "New Deal" was running smoothly, and profits to the men at the top were just starting to pick up a little. In addition to the extra "servicing" the customers were getting, there was added revenue from the sale of pictures, books, films, the stags and the rest, but all that was incidental to the basic commodity offered.

Tony operated in his new position as if it was what he had been made for. He loved the sense of power and importance it gave him. He was the Boss, for all practical purposes; with minor supervision by Angelo, he could hire and fire, hand out jobs or take them away. He thought, happily, that it was like being in Congress or politics and having patronage, handing out postmasterships and judgeships and favors and using his considerable influence. And after all, he told himself, he and most politicians were in pretty much the same line of work when you came right down to it.

The next four months were busy, exciting ones for Tony. He learned that Sharkey had actually done much more than he'd previously thought. There was always something coming up that Tony had to take care of: girls would leave, get married, run off with a pimp, move out of the town or state; new girls would be coming in; there'd be a local mixup about the payoff; medical inspections, records to keep, complaints from a girl or house. Much of this was handled by Leo, Hamlin, or the new man, a husky kid named di Carli, but a large load of it was on Tony's shoulders—and the responsibility for everything that happened rested with him.

But at the end of four months, Tony met his first real trouble. This time it was bad.

He was having dinner about eight P.M., in the apartment with Maria. She had, he thought, become increasingly drawn and worried-looking the last few months. Tony wished he could spend more time with her, but he had to keep on the go, keep up with things. They were halfway through the meal when the phone rang. Tony answered it.

"Tony, this is Angelo. Get up here."

"Your office?"

"Of course, my office. Hurry it up."

"What's the deal? Trouble?"

"Get up here; I'll tell you about it."

Tony hung up and started for the bedroom.

"What's the matter, Tony?" Maria stood up and walked over to him.

"I don't know. Angelo called. Wants to see me; didn't say what for."

She followed him into the bedroom and watched him while he strapped on his gun, then slipped his coat over his heavy shoulders.

"Tony, I hate to see you wear that thing. You're not a cheap thug; why you got to—"

He interrupted, checking his pockets to make sure he had everything. "Look, I usually handle a lot of dough, and sometime I might need this heater. Let's hear no more about it."

"Oh, Tony," she said softly, "I'm just afraid for you. You're too—God, I don't know. But you can't go on like this without no trouble."

"Oh, shut your face, Maria. I got enough troubles, I'll talk to you later." He started out.

"Will you, Tony? Talk to me later about it? I mean seriously. You always tell me to shut up or something. Will you?"

"Yeah, yeah, leave me alone." He left.

Angelo got up when Tony came in. He said, "You've got a job tonight. You know the area around Lafayette Square?"

"Like the back of my hand. What's up?"

"There's two houses out there. On Laguna Street. Not connected with us—I just heard about this an hour ago. They're operating in the open with fifty girls in the two places. They're next door to each other and getting a big play."

"Two places there? I didn't know about them."

"That's the trouble." Angelo stood in front of Tony, bright eyes glaring at him. "You should have known about it, should have stopped it. Now I have to worry about it."

"They're not part of our organization, huh?"

"Of course they're not. The money involved isn't much, but if one group breaks in that's the start." Angelo wheeled around and started pacing the floor. "There's been a slip-up somewhere, a double cross. They're paying off so they can run. You've got to stop it before they get bigger ideas."

"This, uh, this isn't any Syndicate operation, is it?"

"No. I told you I'm independent here in San Francisco. On the prostitution, anyway. There isn't any national tie-up with those two houses. It's a bunch of lousy pimps and a smart operator or two that started this thing."

"You say they're paying off?"

"They have to be. You know these places can't run without a fix, and they've been running two weeks. Romero, I'll handle that part of it. You go out there tonight and close those places up. Either close them or tell them they're now part of our organization and have to contribute the usual fifty percent cut." Angelo started pacing the floor again. Tony had never seen him so worked up.

He wheeled around and walked up to Tony again. "You have a gun on you?"

"Sure."

"There might be trouble. It won't be a picnic. You'd better take some of the boys with you—and look, Romero. Don't mess this up. I want this thing handled as quietly as possible, no mess, understand? Talk to them, tell them they can't possibly buck the established organization—that's me. I don't want any stink about this." He paused and said slowly, "But there might be trouble. They must have expected eventual difficulties with us." He stalked to his desk, pressed a button.

Tony knew that nobody but Angelo had offices here on the tenth floor. Next to this room was another, reached by an adjoining door, in which room there was always at least one, usually more, of Angelo's trusted men. Almost immediately after Angelo pressed the button, the adjoining door was thrown open and Frame hurried in. He stopped inside the room. "Yeah, boss?"

"Kelly in there?"

"Yeah."

"Who else?"

"Just Rock."

"All right. The three of you go with Romero. He'll tell you what to do." Angelo turned to Tony. "You can tell them what to do, can't you?"

"I'll handle it."

"All right." He pointed to the door Frame had come through. "Go that way."

Tony started out and Angelo stopped him. "One thing, Tony. Don't come back here—don't even phone. I don't want any line back to me, just in case. Go straight to your apartment. I'll call you there if I want anything. Here." He fished in his pocket for a square of paper. "This is the address."

Tony took the paper, nodded and went out. The two other men were in the next room. Rock was an immensely broad bruiser, with a face marked up as if from many blows. Kelly was a wasted, anemic-looking kid who couldn't have been more than nineteen. Frame said, "What's up, Tony?"

"I'll tell you in the car. You guys got heaters?"

They nodded. Tony led them out and down to his Buick. He was excited. More excited than it seemed he should be. Part of Angelo's nervousness and energy had been transmitted to him, and then too there was the half-eager, nervous anticipation of what might lie ahead. Shouldn't really be much of a job, he thought. But, as Angelo had said, the guys must have expected trouble when they started up. And this was different from anything Tony had handled up to now.

On the way out to Laguna Street he explained the situation to the three men. Then he said, "We'll handle it like this. We'll walk in like customers—though if any of the guys running the show are around they'll likely recognize me. But we'll try it that way. You guys watch the front and back—you, Rock, and Kelly. Don't let nobody out. Or in. Especially not in, Christ. I didn't get time to case the spot, so there might be other ways in and out; we'll have to chance it. And look, there's a good chance this can be handled quiet, no trouble. For God's sake don't yank out those barkers unless there's real trouble. I'll do the talkin'. With any luck we just walk in, put a panic into whoever's there, and I'll get to the head of the joint and explain the situation. If the guys behind this aren't around, we might have to make some more calls and do a little convincing, but we should tie it up in a couple hours."

Tony knew about where the houses were, but he slowed down and checked the street numbers till he reached the block he wanted. He spotted the two houses, but drove once around the block, then pulled up in front of the houses and cut the engine.

"Here it is. Let's go."

Tony tried the door but it was locked. The three men stood behind him as he rang the bell. In a few seconds a Mexican girl in a white street dress opened the door.

"Evening," Tony said. He started to walk in, but she didn't step aside.

"What you gentlemen want?"

Tony grinned at her. "You know what we want, sweetheart."

"Who was it told you to come here?"

Tony stepped inside, pushing the girl out of his way

and grabbed her wrist. "Look, baby," he said, "you guessed it. This isn't no social call. Now who's the head of this place?"

"I don't know what you mean."

Tony squeezed harder on her wrist and the girl's face twisted. Tony said quietly, "Who here's the boss? Now quick."

She gasped. "Miss Nellie. You're hurtin' my arm."

Tony eased his grip. "Take me to her."

She walked down the hall. Tony went with her saying to Frame, "You come with me. One of you two squat there. Other one check the back."

They walked down the hall, passing a closed door which the Mexican maid said was the parlor. They went into a room on the left of the hall without knocking. A woman in her middle thirties was lying down on a bed in the room, wearing an evening gown.

Tony pushed the girl toward Frame, then walked to the bed and sat down beside the woman as she raised up, startled.

"I'll make this fast," Tony said. "You know goddamn well the merchandise is all sewed up in this town. You been running on the outside. From here on in you're with us, kicking in half, or you're out of business."

The woman leaned back away from him, her hands behind her on the bed. She licked her lips, then said, "Who's 'us'?"

"I'm Tony Romero. That mean anything to you?"

"Oh. I see. I…" she stopped talking. She knew who he was. Fright showed in her face. She looked around the room, then back at Tony.

"Look, Mr. Romero, I just work here."

"How long you been open?"

"Twelve days."

"Who set you up?" She paused. He said, "Quick, dammit. I ain't got all night."

"Fisher."

Tony knew Fisher. Lard Fisher. He was a cheap pimp with a string of half a dozen hookers, some of whom had been in Tony's places. He might be one of the "lousy pimps" Angelo had mentioned, but Tony couldn't imagine him running the show. He said, "What's your name? Your real name."

She looked at his face and shrank a little farther away from him, but she said, "Mrs.…Nelson. That's the truth; you'd find it out if I didn't tell you."

"O.K., Mrs. Nelson. Don't give me no more crap." Tony spoke softly, levelly, staring down at her. "Not if you want to keep your pretty teeth, Mrs. Nelson. Who's the Top in this outfit? And you tell me Fisher again, I'll be disappointed."

She swallowed. "I don't—I can't." She stopped. "It's a cop."

Tony stared at her, not believing for a moment. A cop? Christ, yes. Why not? He'd know the ropes, the ins and outs of the racket, where the payoff went. He'd pull plenty of weight. Tony's thoughts were interrupted by noises in the hall outside; shouts and yells.

Suddenly there was the sharp, unmistakable crack of a gun, then another shot. Tony jumped to his feet.

Frame had already run into the hall; Tony reached for his revolver, raced to the door with the gun in his hand. He paused in the darker hall, pressed against the wall while his eyes became accustomed to the more gloomy interior here. A door burst open opposite him as a woman somewhere in the house screamed. A fat geezer ran out of the room opposite, pulling at his pants. His face was sagging and misshapen with fright. A completely nude girl stepped to the door, slammed it. A key turned in the lock. Tony started toward the front door gripping his gun. A woman in negligee raced through the door of the parlor and ran toward the back of the house, screaming, her mouth wide open. She ran by Tony, still screaming. Tony couldn't see any of the three men who'd come with him. Where the hell were those bastards?

He felt a tingling excitement running through him, like the time he'd hammered in Alterie's face, a little like the feeling he'd had the night Shark had been murdered. He ran toward the open door of the parlor as a man leaped through it into the hallway. Tony saw the dull gleam of light from a gun in the man's hand. The man wasn't Frame or Rock or Kelly. The guy stopped, stared at Tony.

"Romero!" he yelled. "You son of a bitch!" He yanked up his gun.

For a fraction of a second Tony hesitated. He didn't know the guy, had never seen him, but the guy knew him. Must be one of the men running this spot. As if the motions were slowed down to half their normal speed, Tony in his heart-pounding excitement saw the other man's gun swing up, point at him. Tony jumped to his right, slamming into the far wall as the gun in the hand of the man ten feet away blasted at him, flame spurting from the muzzle. Tony felt the light touch at the shoulder of his coat, saw the spurt of flame, heard the slug smack into the wall far behind him, and then his own gun roared in his hand, leaped upward, then was pulled down and steadied by his muscles, roared again. Tony's mind was filled with a maelstrom of impressions and flashing thoughts. He hadn't been conscious of pulling the trigger, yet its roar was still ringing in his ears. The other man had staggered backwards, was clawing at the wall, sliding down it now.

Tony ran toward him, stopped alongside him as the man toppled forward from his knees and lay still. There was a faint smear of blood on the wall where he had slid down it. Tony stared at him, breathing through his open mouth, still uncomprehending. He looked at the Magnum in his right fist, then knelt and felt for the man's pulse. There was no pulse, no heartbeat. Tony rolled him over and saw the two small bullet holes, one over the heart, the other far down in the man's groin. He was dead.

Feverishly, hardly knowing why he did it, Tony knelt by the dead man, went through his pockets. There was a thick roll of bills in the right trousers pocket; nothing else of importance. No wallet, no identification, no cards. Only a comb and file, and the money.

He heard a step behind him and whirled, swinging the gun up. He stopped just in time. It was Frame.

Tony stood up. "What the hell happened? Who started this sonofabitch of a mess?" Tony's voice was loud.

Frame looked down at the man on the floor. "Him maybe. I don't know. Somebody sapped Kelly—" he pointed toward the base of the front door—"then came on inside, I guess." Frame's voice was level, but pitched higher than usual, stretched with suppressed excitement. He held a heavy automatic in his right hand, waving it back and forth nervously.

Tony looked at the door, at the floor in front of it. He hadn't even seen Kelly crumpled up there. "You sure he's just sapped?"

"Yeah. I seen him when I busted out here."

"Where's Rock?"

"In back with Fisher. After I checked Kelly here I run into the parlor. Fish—I didn't know who he was right then, hadn't seen his face—was runnin' toward the back. Rock caught him there and I bounced Betsy—" he waved the gun—"off his squash. Rock's watchin' him. He's hurt."

"Rock?"

"Yeah. Slug in his shoulder. From him, I guess." Frame pointed his gun at the dead man. "I didn't get the straight of it. He winged Rock then busted out this way. I come after him soon's I popped Fish." He licked his lips. "You beat me to him. He's dead?"

"Yeah. He took a shot at me. I...let him have it. Christ, I had to. Who the hell is he?"

"Dunno. Never seen him. He's nobody now."

A woman tried to run by them and reach the front door. Her face was white. Tony grabbed her.

"Get the hell back in your room." He glanced down the hall. Three other women and a man with no shoes on were coming toward them. Tony shoved the girl back the way she'd come and faced the others, standing with his legs spread apart. "Get back in the rooms! All of you." He held the gun up in his raised hand like a club. "Go on, move. Nobody leaves here."

They stopped, milled around like sheep, went back. Tony turned to Frame. "Christ, what a mess. How about the back?"

"There's where Rock is. And Fish. Say, Rock needs a sawbones. He's plenty tough, but there's that slug in his shoulder."

"Rock'll keep a few minutes. And we got to tie this up, Frame. It's a big enough mess already. Jesus Christ! Angelo's gonna turn inside out. Oh, crap, what a goddamn mess this is." He paused, licked his lips, thinking. "Frame, round up everybody. Everybody still here. Herd them all in the parlor—no, check the men, and if you're sure they're just customers take their names and get rid of them. We got to settle this fast. Damn, we still got the other spot next to here."

Frame sucked on his teeth. "Ain't we gonna get outa here, Tony? Somethin'…might happen. Maybe cops. Somebody must of heard all the racket."

Kelly groaned, started moving.

"Get those people in the parlor, Frame. Then see how Kelly is. I'll be in the parlor. Snap it up."

Frame hurried off and started pounding on doors as Tony went through the parlor and found a door leading from its far wall through another hallway lined with rooms. He walked down it to a closed door at the rear of the house. Rock stood there, one hand pressed against his shoulder, red lines of blood curling around his fingers. Another man, Lard Fisher, was crumpled on the floor.

"Rock," Tony said. "How you makin' it?"

"Not too bad. What's goin' on?"

Tony shook his head. It seemed everybody wondered that, himself included. All of a sudden, bang, all hell broke loose. Guns going off and naked babes running around and guys without pants. It looked now like there'd been only Fisher and the dead guy raising hell.

"I think it's over," he said. "Can you hang on a little longer, Rock? I'd like to get you patched up now, but we got to settle this mess while we're here. Only take maybe five minutes."

"I'm O.K. Don't even hurt yet. I'm good for half an hour."

Tony stepped to the back door, opened it and looked out. There was an alley there that he'd spotted when they first drove up and circled the block before coming in.

"Rock, can you handle a car like you are?"

"Yah. This won't bother me much for a while. Didn't catch the bone. What happened to that sonofabitch?"

"I popped him. He's...dead."

"Good. I missed him."

"Get the car off the street. Bring it around to the alley. We may have to jump for it yet."

"What about him?" Rock nudged Fisher with his foot. Fisher groaned, starting to come to.

"Hell." Tony ground his teeth together, then pulled the gun from under his coat. He reversed it, bent over and carefully hit Fisher on the back of his head. "He'll keep for a while—we'll take him with us. Get the car."

They went back to the parlor and Rock went on out

the front while Tony looked around. There were about twenty girls and two men. Didn't look as if anybody had got out. Frame stood by the door; Kelly was sitting in a chair, his head in his hands.

Tony walked to Frame's side. "Who're the two guys?"

"Don't know. No identification, so I kept them for you to look at. I got rid of nine others. They all seemed O.K. Hoped they was."

"Get their names and where they live?"

"Sure," Frame tapped his coat pocket. "Just in case."

Tony walked over in front of the two men. Nervousness was building in him, jumping in his stomach. They had to get out of here. "Who are you guys?" he asked harshly.

They told him, nervously, giving names that might have been theirs, might have been fake.

Tony turned and looked at the silent women. "O.K., you pigs. I guess you know your little factory's gone sour. Now who knows these guys here? Speak up. I got no spare time."

One of the girls bit her lip and said hesitatingly, "I know...that one." She pointed. "He's been here a couple times."

"You know what I mean. I don't want no customers; I want the guys put you in here."

"I know. He's all right. Just a customer."

Another girl vouched for the same guy, and three

girls identified the other as only a customer. There wasn't much Tony could do about it if they were lying, but he figured they were telling the truth. They'd all had their pants scared off. Some of them looked ready to pass out.

Tony shoved the two men out the front door, then turned to the women. "You know who I am, some of you," he said. "I'm Tony Romero. Nobody hustles in town unless I say so." He stopped. "Frame, you and Kelly get next door, see what's up over there." They went out. Tony said, "O.K., the place is closed." He looked around the room till he saw Mrs. Nelson. "Get this. You can work for us, and kick in—or not work at all. I'll fix it so you can't get a job sorting garbage, not in Frisco. Make up your minds fast. Now, who's this bastard cop? And who else set this up?"

Mrs. Nelson licked her lips, then jerked her head toward the door. Tony whirled around, but nobody was there. Then he heard it: the distant, nerve-tingling wail of sirens. At the same moment Frame ran in, closely followed by Kelly.

"Cops," he said. "Hear 'em? They might not feel like talkin'."

Tony knew what he meant. They might be "wrong" cops who'd haul them all down to the can, or there might even be shooting.

Frame went on, "Next door's all shut up. Nobody there. Must have beat it when the noise started."

Tony swore softly. "Get out back," he said. "Rock's got the car there."

They ran toward the back as the sirens screamed closer. Tony paused only long enough to say, "You pigs are out of business—come see me if you want to work. You can find me. And you damn well better."

He was talking disjointedly, in a kind of crazy way, he knew, but the jumping excitement in him was like little explosions in his blood. He was all charged up, as if he'd been sucking on reefers. He glanced once around the room then ran to the back door. The car was waiting, motor idling. He jumped in and said, "Step on it." The sirens were almost upon them now. "Get this heap moving."

Tony let himself into his apartment. It was nearly midnight. They'd taken Rock to a doctor after they got out of the alley barely ahead of the coppers.

Tony went inside, and headed for the bar in his front room, the lights were still on. He poured two fingers of bourbon into a glass and was squirting soda into it when Maria came in from the bedroom. She was still fully clothed, in a green silk dress.

"Tony," she said, "what's the matter? Angelo's called half a dozen times. What did you have to go out for tonight?"

"Angelo? What'd he want?"

"He wants you to call him. Tony, you look funny.

You look sick. You all right?" Her face was worried, drawn with strain. "I been going crazy, honey." She walked around beside him, hugged his arm.

"I'm O.K. I better call Angelo."

"Tony, what happened?"

"I'll tell you later." He walked over to the phone and dialed Angelo's office number. When he answered Tony said, "This is Tony. Maria says you called here."

"You idiot. You know who you killed? A cop. A god-damn cop. The whole town's going crazy. The D.A. called me; the Mayor called me. You've really got the heat on now. Get up here."

Chapter Eleven

Frame and Kelly were with Angelo when Tony arrived at the office. Tony shut the door behind him and walked over to the desk behind which Angelo was sitting. Angelo looked up at Tony with his yellowish eyes hard.

"You fixed things good, Romero. The town's like a hornet's nest."

Tony leaned forward, his hands flat on the desk top. "What's the matter with you? I never heard you talk like this before. That trigger-happy yentzer tossed a pill at me. I'm supposed to catch it in my teeth? Hell, he just got through plugging Rock. I didn't go there to shoot the guy; it just happened."

"All right, all right. I know, Romero. Frame and Kelly told me about it. But there's hell to pay now."

"He was running the house. His pals on the force will find that out soon enough. When that hits the papers—"

Angelo laughed. Then he stopped laughing abruptly and dug into his desk for a cigar. "His pals on the force," he mimicked. "I keep forgetting how innocent you are underneath, Romero. The morning papers will say that a noble, fearless, honest officer of the vice squad was shot in cold blood by a hoodlum. There'll be references to houses of ill fame and intimations that the fearless Sergeant Jorgensen was investigating undercover vice, killed in the line of duty." Angelo stuck the unlighted cigar in his mouth and chewed on it viciously. "Every drooling preacher in town is going to start screaming about White Slavers and the poor, innocent girls forced into lives of shame.

"And listen, Romero." Angelo's voice dropped lower as he leaned forward across the desk, looking seriously at Tony. "No matter what kind of slimy, no-good bastard Jorgensen was, he was still a cop. All cops are pure—when they get killed. Jorgensen is the next name on the Honor Roll of the San Francisco Police Department; you can depend on that. And the one crime cops have to solve is a cop kill. If they didn't, cops would get knocked off like ordinary citizens. So... Jorgensen's fellow police officers *must* get his killer. It's simple self-defense."

Tony ground his teeth together. He was mad, furious, but he didn't really know what to be mad at. Angelo? The cops? The lousy world? Himself? The mess was even worse than he'd figured, even if he hadn't been able to think about it much yet.

"O.K., he said. "What's next, then? I'm not gonna go down and say, 'I did it; beat the hell out of me.' So what happens?"

"You get out of town. Tonight. I know how these things work, Tony." Angelo's voice was a little calmer. "They'll get the killer; and he'll probably be convicted, sentenced, maybe even sent to the gas chamber. But, Tony, it doesn't have to be you."

Tony fished in his pockets, nervously got out a cigarette and lit up. "It better not be me," he said.

Angelo's eyes narrowed slightly. "You leave tonight. This is the situation, Tony. While you're out of town, you're no good to me here. But we always need new girls for the houses. Particularly now that you've done such a good job of picking up business. I've been meaning to compliment you on that, Tony. Out of town, you should be able to find many girls who'd be glad to start life anew, shall we say, in the big city."

Tony frowned. The guy wanted him to go out pandering, procuring fresh babes for the houses.

Angelo noted the frown and asked, "Something troubling you? You don't have any moral scruples about it, do you?"

"It's not that. I never done it; maybe I wouldn't be much good."

Angelo said matter-of-factly, "You're good-looking, Tony, and you've got a big car, plenty of money. You don't need anything else. You know that most of the girls we get come to us of their own free will, because they want to make more money than they make picking berries or milking cows or whatever such creatures do. You've shown your initiative and intelligence already, Tony. I have confidence in you."

That was great. Angelo had confidence in him. Angelo wasn't the guy that had to work on the dames. But what the hell; there wasn't much choice.

"O.K.," Tony said. "I'll check out tonight. But, dammit, things were just goin' good here. I hate to blow."

They talked another half hour, then Tony left. Angelo figured the heat would die down in a couple months, maybe sooner if the cops caught their killer. In the meantime Tony was to recruit what girls he could and send them to Frisco. They'd get in touch with Leo, who was taking over in Tony's enforced absence. That part Tony didn't like at all, but Leo was to stay on his own salary, and Tony would continue to get his one-tenth cut of the organization's fifty percent of the gross. It would be, in many ways, like a vacation with pay. And, Tony thought, he could use a month or two to relax in. He'd been pushing himself pretty hard.

By the time he got back to his apartment, he was feeling pretty good about it.

Maria was sitting up in the front room, a drink in her hand. Maria; she might not like this angle.

She got up and came to him. "How...how is it?"

"O.K. I told you it'd be O.K., didn't I?"

"Really, Tony? You wouldn't kid me?"

"Straight goods. It's gonna be all right."

Relief washed over her face. "Oh, I'm glad!" She held up the drink, smiling. "Look. I had to do something; I was going to get blind. I was worried sick. I had four drinks, can't feel a one." Her face brightened. "Tony, let's just you and me get drunk. Right here in the apartment. Like old times, when we first seen each other again."

"Hell, baby. I'd like to. Really I would. But I can't. I told you everything'll be O.K.—and it will—but I got to skip town a while. Till the heat's off. Honey, the panic is really on; you'd think I popped Li'l Abner."

She was quiet for a few seconds. "You have to leave? Leave town?"

"Uh-huh."

"But *Tony,* what about me?"

"Hell, it won't be for long, sweetheart. Maybe a month."

"Can I go with you?"

"Well…it wouldn't work. I'll be movin' around a lot. I'll be callin' you all the time; maybe I can sneak into town."

She bit her lip and stared at him curiously. "I don't think you want me with you."

"What the hell kind of talk's that? Sure I want you with me. Ain't I wanted you with me for two years and more? But I got to lie low, be free to move. I didn't mention it, but the guy the trouble's about is a cop. Was."

Her shoulders slumped. "You don't want me with you."

"Well, Jesus Christ. Didn't you hear me? I said I shot a cop."

"I hear you." She went to the bar and began mixing a drink. "You want one?"

"Yeah, I could stand one. Don't put no poison in it."

"Sometimes, Tony, just for a little minute, I think I'd like to. Something slow and awful." She turned around with the two drinks and smiled slightly. "Well, here's to…to success, Tony." She gave him his drink.

Napa's best hotel, Tony thought ruefully, wasn't much like the St. Francis or the Mark Hopkins. Napa was a quiet, peaceful little town—and there wasn't much for the girls to do in a place like this. Except, of course, what girls do everywhere. He had driven straight here from San Francisco, arriving about three o'clock in the morning. He'd chosen Napa because it was close to Frisco, and a good spot to spend a couple days while he planned his next moves. Napa was a famous wine-growing country, too, and many of Tony's fellow Italians lived here and in the nearby towns.

Angelo, in that last talk with Tony had said, "Hit the smaller cities where there's some unemployment, or where the pay is poor; go to the dull, dead spots where the girls get bored and maybe dream about the big city. You'll do best among the poor and the ignorant, girls that are hard up for money, or men—or love, Tony. Find the girls that aren't happy at home, don't get along with their folks, and you've got a shipment." Angelo paused, then went on in a businesslike manner, "You'll have to handle it your own way, naturally, but don't be afraid to flash your roll—keep a big roll handy. And, one other thing, the younger they are, the better."

Tony was thinking about that now in his "suite" at the Plaza Hotel, the suite consisting of a sitting room, bedroom, and bath. The younger the better, huh? Might as well get started, he thought. It was two o'clock in the afternoon.

He had coffee in two cafes. Neither the coffee or the waitresses were any good. In the third spot, the coffee was lousy, but the waitress was a sharp little gal with bold eyes. Built, too, thought Tony, letting his eyes roam over her breasts and waist and hips as she stood in front of him. She was young, but she looked wise.

"Coffee," he said.

"That all?" He nodded, and she said, "Big spender, huh?"

She walked down to the gleaming coffee urn and filled a heavy white porcelain cup, brought it back. "Here's your coffee, sport." There was only one other customer in the small spot at this hour. The cafe itself was only a counter with eight stools, and three tables along the opposite wall. The girl leaned against the counter and looked at him.

"Why aren't you in school, sweetheart?" he asked.

"Listen to him. Sweetheart. You sure ain't from this town, are you?"

"No. I'm from...out of town."

"I don't go to school. I graduated."

Tony had parked his Buick convertible, gleaming from a fresh polish job, directly in front of the cafe window. She glanced casually at it, then back at him. "That yours?"

"Yeah."

"Some boat."

"Year old now. Figure on gettin' a new one. Maybe you'll help me pick it out. I'm a stranger in town."

She moistened her lips. "Maybe."

Tony took one swallow of his coffee and got up. He carried his money in his pants pocket now; a lot of the Frisco sharpies did that. He pulled the thick roll, held together with a rubber band, from his pocket, snapped off the band and pulled a five from the inside of the roll. He tossed it on the counter, snapped the rubber back on the bills and thrust them carelessly into his pocket.

She said, "Coffee no good?"

"Terrible. Well, I'll see you later, sweetheart."

She walked to the cash register at the end of the

counter. "I'm cashier, too." She rang up ten cents, then said, "Here's your change."

"Keep it. Look, honey, what's a guy do in this dump for amusement?" He paused by the cash register.

"Keep *all* the change?"

"Sure. Anything on in town?"

She stared at him. "Well...ain't much to do. There's a dance in Hall's Hall tonight. Not much, but it's something."

"Want to go?"

"With you?"

"No, by yourself. Hell, yes, with me."

"I got a date."

"Can't you break it?"

"Well..." She glanced out at the Buick, then at Tony's face. "O.K."

"Tell this Joe I'm an old friend. From Frisco." He grinned at her.

"That's funny; that's his name, Joe," she said.

"Where'll I pick you up?"

She frowned. "Why'nt I meet you downtown?"

"Sure." Tony thought about it a minute. What the hell, he might as well press his luck. "Listen, sweetheart," he said, "I just pulled in here last night; not much sleep. I'm gonna take a nap first—so I'll be fresh tonight. When you get off here?"

"Five."

"I'm at the Plaza. Number twenty-four. Why don't you come up? We can take off from there."

She hesitated. "I don't know."

He squinted at her. "Oh, I get it. That's a sin in a hick town, huh?" He laughed.

"What's so funny? O.K., I'll see you later."

"Twenty-four. Just come on up." He went out. Maybe she wouldn't show. So what? And maybe she would.

Promptly at seven o'clock she knocked on the door. Tony was showered and shaved, dressed except for his shirt. He opened the door and stood bare-chested, looking out at her. "Hi, sweetheart. Come on in. I'll be ready in a minute."

She walked by him and he pointed to the couch. "Sit down." She was wearing a blue crepe dress that fit her tightly and buttoned down the front. It was a cheesy dress, Tony thought, and there was too much makeup on her face, but she looked good. "Say," he said, "you really look beautiful. You're gonna knock their eyes out tonight."

She smiled, pleased. "Quit pullin' my leg. Say, I don't even know your name."

"Tony."

"Tony what?"

"Just Tony. How about you?"

"Ruth."

He walked to the dresser and picked up a pack of cigarettes next to a bottle of whiskey. He gave her a cigarette, lit it and asked, "Want a drink while I finish getting dressed?"

"I don't care."

He walked to the dresser. "I got nothing but bourbon," he said. "Some Coke. Want Coke with it?" She said O.K. and he mixed two drinks with stiff slugs of bourbon, put in ice cubes he'd got from the bellhop, and gave her the tall glass. There was enough whiskey in the long glass for four ordinary drinks.

While he put on his shirt, they talked, a little stiffly at first, but by the time Tony had his tie on and was ready to leave, the conversation was freer. She had apparently been ill at ease in his room, but the conversation and half the drink made her seem more comfortable.

Tony sat down by her on the couch. "We got a little time to kill. Let's have one more highball and take off." He grinned. "We ought to be real peppy by the time we get to the shindig."

"O.K., I don't mind." Tony tilted his glass, finished the drink, and she did the same. He made the next ones a little weaker. Didn't want the doll getting sick.

Finally he said, "Ruth, how old are you, anyway? Makes no difference to me if you're nine or twenty-nine. I'm curious."

Her eyes were a trifle dulled. "You really wanna know, Tony?" He nodded. "Well, I'm sixteen."

"No kidding? You look lots older than that, Ruth. I thought you were around twenty-one."

She liked that. "You're nice, Tony. I'm glad you come in today."

"Me too. We've got to see a lot of each other." He put his arm around her shoulder, moved toward her on the couch and pulled her gently against him. She moistened her lips.

They got to the dance at ten o'clock. Ruth danced close to him, insinuating her body against his, her previous reserve vanished now. A guy asked her for a dance and she said to Tony, "Do you mind?"

"Don't be silly, Ruth." He grinned. "Why would I mind?"

They'd been at the dance about half an hour then, and he and Ruth had talked to several of her friends, briefly. In a small town like Napa, Tony, a good-looking, sharply dressed guy from out of town, was something out of the ordinary, interesting. He spotted one of Ruth's girlfriends, a slim thing almost as tall as Tony himself, and asked her to dance. They chatted casually for one number and, when they talked, she leaned away from him to look at his face while keeping her hips pressed close against him. Tony was to learn that many of the girls here—and in a number of other small towns—danced the same way, or with variations which amounted to the same thing. There were a number of stag girls and guys present.

It was a fair six-piece orchestra, and the floor was good. Most of the girls were in their teens, but some of them were really attractive. And there was the inevitable sprinkling of pure horrors. Tony was having a pretty good time. He took the slim girl back to her seat, spent a short intermission drinking a Coke with Ruth, then the music started again and a character danced off with her. Tony looked around. Three girls were standing at the end of the Coke bar, talking. They were all damn nice looking, he thought. Two of them especially. The third one was a kind of half-pretty gal, a couple inches over five feet tall and with soot-black hair that hung down to her shoulders. Tony walked over to the three of them. No sense sitting out the dance. Either one of those two sharp ones would do fine.

But Tony surprised himself by stopping by the three girls and asking the black-haired one, "Dance, honey?"

She looked up at him, and he saw her full face for the first time. She was a sweet-looking tomato. He wondered how she'd dance. Close and cozy like the last one? She didn't look like the type, somehow. She had the shape for it, but it didn't fit the face. She'd probably want to waltz two feet apart. What the hell had he asked this pig for?

She smiled sweetly. "No, thank you."

"Huh?" Tony hadn't even considered the possibility of her refusing. "You already got this dance, honey?"

She frowned slightly, then smiled again. "No. Do you call everybody honey?"

He blinked. Here was another one of these characters that talked screwy. "Not everybody," he said finally. And for some perverse reason he added, "Just the sexy ones."

She turned her head slightly and looked at him from the corner of her eyes, no amusement in them. All of a sudden he wished he hadn't said that. It sounded crude and out of place. She began talking to the other girls, paying no attention to Tony. Why, the little bitch, he thought. Who the hell did she think she was?

"Hey," he said suddenly. The word popped out and as she turned toward him he didn't yet know what else he was going to say. She looked at him coolly, from blue eyes. He said, "What's your name?"

She sighed. "Betty. Now will you go away?"

"Well I'll be goddamned."

She laughed suddenly, merrily, obviously amused by his discomfort. "Look," she said in more friendly fashion, "there's a hundred girls to dance with here. If you *must* dance, maybe June or Vi would like to. Or anybody."

June and Vi were apparently the two with her. One

of them, a striking blonde about nineteen, looked at Tony, smiling broadly.

Tony said, "Hell, I'm scared to ask anybody else now."

The blonde said, "Don't be."

He shrugged. "O.K., a man don't live but once. You think maybe, possibly, perhaps, we might dance? Together, I mean."

She chuckled. "Why, I'd *love* to."

"You June or Vi?"

"I'm June."

"O.K., come on," he said. "Come on, honey. Where you work?"

"Westburns. Little record and bookstore. Come in and I'll sell you a book."

"O.K. Save me one with pictures."

She smiled slowly. "What kind of pictures?"

He grinned. "Pictures of animals," he said. "I'm crazy about animals."

"I'll bet."

"This Betty chill works there too, huh?"

"Yes. What's the matter, you interested in her? She's kind of cute, isn't she?"

"Nah, she's a plain Jane. Looks like if you patted her fanny she'd think she needed an abortion."

June shook her head. "You sure have a blunt way of talking."

"I'm a blunt guy."

When the dance was over Tony took her back to the Coke bar. Vi was still there, sitting in a wooden chair against the wall, but Tony didn't see Betty. He felt oddly disappointed. He thanked June and she sat down by Vi. "We'll have to try that again after a while," he said.

Later on, he left her. About time he found Ruth. For all he knew she was out in the hay somewhere, squealing like a stuck pig. Christ, she was some squealer. He walked around until he spotted her on the dance floor.

The next morning they had breakfast in the room. Tony had learned that Ruth lived with an older, married sister. Her parents were dead. It wouldn't be too bad if she stayed all night with him; she'd been away all night before. She'd just get a bawling out, is all. Tony had told her she might as well live here with him for a while. Hell, they'd have a great time. He'd buy her some new clothes; she could get rid of those old rags. Well, she'd said, gee, maybe.

He left her in the rooms in the afternoon.

"Where you going, Tony?"

"Just look around a little."

"You hurry back and bring me a kiss."

"Yeah, sure."

He went out. Christ, she made him sick. And she was too easy. She was like a machine. Press the right

button and she turned over. "How about it, baby?"
"O.K." Nuts. That had been some deal last night. The
start with Ruth. Then the dance. Vi and June. And that
Betty. What a frigid piece she was. Imagine her not
dancing with me, he thought. Too good for the
common man, I suppose. I should of kicked her in
the butt.

Jesus, he needed a drink. And he'd had enough of
that Ruth. He ought to just put it to her straight and
let her take it or leave it. Get out of this town; hit
Fresno or Sacramento, someplace where there was
some life. Hell, he'd only been here a little over a day.
What was the matter with him? He wondered what
was going on in Frisco, what the cops were doing.

He didn't really expect to find a San Francisco
paper, but in a little cigar store a block from the main
drag he found what he wanted. The gray-haired atten-
dant dug into a stack of papers under the counter and
pulled out today's and yesterday's Frisco papers.
Behind the cigar stand was a pool hall and small,
crummy bar. Tony took the papers to the bar and
ordered a scotch and water.

"We got nothing but wine and beer," the bartender said.

"Gimme a beer then."

He looked at yesterday's paper first. They'd given
it the works, the full treatment. The panic was really
on for sure. Big black headlines blared: POLICEMAN

MURDERED. The sub leads might have been written by Angelo himself; he'd called the turn. The story stated that Sergeant Jorgensen, vice-squad officer with a long and honorable record of brilliant and faithful service, had been murdered during an investigation of alleged prostitution and narcotics smuggling. He was known to have been in possession of important information damaging to many of the top racketeers of the city. Careful references were made to the Mafia, and a national Crime Syndicate. The killer was a local hoodlum and the police were aware of his identity. They expected an arrest within 48 hours.

The later paper had headlines about the sad state of the world at large, but the murder of Jorgensen, that brilliant scourge of crime (with an IQ of 75), still occupied much of the front page and pages inside. More photographs today, too, of the houses Jorgensen had been investigating. Yesterday there'd been a nice picture of the body.

Tony drank his beer, left the papers on the bar and went out. It was funny, he thought, but he didn't feel much one way or another about the kill. It was almost as if it hadn't involved him personally, as if it were merely something he'd read about. Two months away from the home town; that was a hell of a time. He found himself wishing the cops would hurry up and pin the job on somebody.

He stood in the sunlight outside the cigar store, wondering what to do with himself. Recruit some whores; crap. He grinned wryly. He'd started out in the racket pretty high up, worked his way almost to the top. Here he was now, practically a male streetwalker, working on the babes. He'd worked his way up to pimp.

He stood on the sidewalk for a moment, then swore, turned and went back in.

"Hey, pop," he said to the gray-haired guy. "Where's a place called Westburns? Some kind of book store."

The man gave him directions and Tony started walking. Maybe that June had been thinking about the big dough he'd mentioned. Might as well see what she had to say.

Chapter Twelve

Westburns was a small place on the main drag. Betty stood behind the counter, and she glanced up at him as he came in.

He'd been thinking about her, rather than June, as he walked down the street. All he could remember about her—except for that last look as he and Ruth left the dance hall—was her black, long hair, and her blue eyes. He saw her even more clearly now than he had last night. Her nose was straight, narrow. Her lips were full and red, the mouth wide. She had high, prominent cheekbones, and maybe, thought Tony, that was what gave her the haughty air she had, that snooty look. There wasn't a damn thing sensual about her face except maybe the generous lips and mouth. Her face, he decided, wasn't pretty. But maybe you could call it striking. Her skin was so white and smooth that it made her black hair look blacker, her mouth more vivid. She wasn't smiling as she looked at him.

Tony walked over to the counter, feeling an inexplicable nervousness that was foreign to him. "Hello, Betty."

"Hello."

He couldn't think of anything to say for a moment. Then, "Uh, is June around?"

"Uh-huh. She's in the booth. Sometimes when it's slow like this we take turns listening to records."

He wished she'd quit looking at him so solemn like that; it was making him feel funny, exposed, as if he were standing there naked, casually passing the time of day. You couldn't tell what she was thinking from her face.

They stood facing each other on opposite sides of the counter for half a minute, then Tony said, "Well, I just came in to say hello to June. She's in back, huh?"

Betty nodded.

He walked toward the rear of the store and up to the booth. He could hear the music softly, a jazzy number with plenty of hot, brassy trumpet. That June was a pretty brassy number herself. He looked in the glass window of the door. June was sitting in the cushioned seat, her legs apart and her dress up over her knees, the cloth sagging down between her legs. A hand rested on each thigh and she was keeping time to the music with an index finger of each hand. Her head rested on the cushion behind her, eyes closed, bright blonde hair bunched on her shoulders, half smile on her face.

He tapped on the glass.

She jerked her head around, eyes opening wide. He saw her lips form "Tony!" but he couldn't hear the words. She smiled. Then she crooked her finger at him, motioning him inside. He opened the door and stepped into the small booth, clicked the door shut behind him.

"Hi, Tony. I didn't think you'd be around."

"Said I would. Turn that thing down."

She turned a dial and the music became soft instead of the raucous blaring it had been. "Sit down." She patted the seat at her side. There was barely room for two people, and sitting there June's thigh was pressed tightly against his own.

"I'm glad you came," she said. "It's sure dead today."

"Still dead?"

"Not now it isn't." She grinned. "Kind of close in here, isn't it, Tony?"

"Not too close. Could be closer."

"Tony, I'll tell you something. I sit in here and listen to these hot records, these hot licks, and it makes me hot. It makes me hotter than hell. You ever get like that?"

"Not from records."

"I wouldn't talk like this, but—well, last night. We're sort of like old friends, aren't we?"

"Sure, June."

"Oh, Jesus, I'm hot."

The way she was babbling was making Tony a little hot. He said, "Maybe I should have had a trumpet with me last night."

"You didn't need one, Tony. But—this is different.

Funny different. There's a dozen kids in town the same way; once in a while we get together and put on some hot records and really go. It gets right down inside you."

Tony grinned. "That sounds real good. Think I'd like that."

"You nut. Oh, *listen* to that!" She turned up the volume a little, stretched her legs out in front of her and squirmed slightly, rolling back and forth on her hips. "Doesn't that *do* something to you, Tony?"

"What you're doing does. Last night I kept thinking about the way you finish dances."

She sat up straight again. "That was the idea." She looked at him. "Remember the little fun we had in the corner?" Her voice was soft, intimate.

"Sure I remember."

She looked at him. Finally she said, "Do I have to draw you a picture?"

"Hell, there's a big glass window in this door, June. You want people watching?"

They sat quietly for three or four minutes. Tony said, "Tell you something, June. A gal as full of hell as you, it seems a shame you don't get anything but kicks out of it."

Her head was bent down as she listened to the records, blonde hair falling forward in front of her face. She looked sideways at him. "What could I get besides kicks?" Tony could hardly hear her, the music was so loud.

"I mentioned something about it last night. Money, I mean."

She kept looking at him, red tongue curling out again to touch her upper lip. Then she looked away from him, down at the floor again, listened to a throaty alto sax.

In a couple minutes Tony said, "I've got to beat it. I'll see you later, June."

She sat up. "I want to see you, too. Tony, a little more before you go? A little bit?"

He grinned at her. "Later, honey." He went out. He stopped at the counter where Betty was reading a book. "So long," he said.

She looked at him from cool blue eyes. "You've got somebody's lipstick on."

He'd forgotten about that. He pulled out a white handkerchief and scrubbed his mouth. Confused, he said, "Don't you ever lose any of yours?"

She dropped her gaze to his mouth for a moment, then looked back at his eyes. She didn't say anything. She started reading her book again.

Tony stared at her, frowned. "Jesus Christ," he said. "That must be a damned interesting book. What is it, a Bible?"

She didn't look up. "Why do you swear so much?" she asked.

He didn't know quite how to answer such a stupid question. "Hell," he said, "why not?"

There wasn't any more conversation, and Tony left. He walked down the street thinking. Thinking about himself, which was something Tony Romero rarely did. As for the night with Ruth, and what had just gone on with June in the record booth, he didn't feel there was anything wrong or immoral or bad about what he'd done. And, actually, there was no logical reason why he should have thought so. But, he kept thinking, that business with June. He felt a little funny about it. And the reason was that he couldn't help thinking Betty wouldn't have liked knowing what was happening back there. She'd probably have felt it was pretty terrible. And, even as the thought rose in his mind, he was puzzled that he should be considering Betty's attitude at all.

Three days in this stinking burg. Three long, lousy days in this dead town—and with Ruth on his neck all the time. I kick your teeth in, Ruthie. Drop dead, Ruthie. Ruthie, you know what? You stink, Ruthie. How in hell did she get so nauseating in only sixteen years?

Tony walked down the main drag, turned and went to the pool hall. He ordered a beer at the little bar, then another. He told the bartender to keep the beer coming till he slid off the stool.

Friday afternoon. A stinking, lousy, dismal Friday afternoon. Frig Friday. Saturday coming up, Saturday night, the big night in Napa. All kinds of excitement:

taffy pulls, window shopping, read books. Oh, sonof-abitch. Napa, the rip of creation, and he was stuck in it. God, to be back in Frisco. Tony had been away from San Francisco before, but always he'd known he'd be home again in a day or two—and even then he'd missed it. This might stretch into a couple months or more. He wanted to call Angelo, but he was to phone only on Saturday nights. He felt like getting in the Buick and heading for town, driving down Market, walking the streets. He could imagine himself walking down the little alleys with Betty, ferreting out the small out-of-the-way restaurants and bars hidden away off the streets. Getting one of the dark booths in the back of the room, a drink before dinner. He stopped, frowned. He'd done it again. Betty again. This wasn't the first time he'd caught himself thinking about her, about going places, doing things with Betty. He shook his head, drank his umpteenth beer. Yeah, Tony, he said to himself, you better get out of this trap. You're losing your marbles.

He shook off his mood. "Hey, bartender," he called. "Fill it up. Have one on me."

"Well, don't mind if I do. Thanks."

"This is a metropolis," said Tony. "This is the great heart of the wine belt. Where in hell is the heart of the whiskey belt?"

The bartender looked at him oddly. He poured two beers.

"You're new around here, ain't you, fellow?"

"I'm old around here. I'm old and gray. Tell you something. I have expired. I'm dead."

"Aw," said the bartender.

"Say, when does the next exciting thing happen?"

"Huh? Say, fellow, I don't know what you mean."

Tony shook his head. "I know. I don't know why I asked. I'm sick of beer. Give me a bourbon."

"Look, fellow, you know I got no bourbon. Take it easy."

"Give me a bourbon before I wreck this place. I'll throw it out on the street."

The bartender licked his lips. "Hey, now. Don't get rambunctious. I don't wanna have to call the cops."

"Rambunctious," Tony repeated. "Oh, great. Stretch my galluses. Cops?" Tony laughed loudly. "Cops?" He reached into his pants pocket and pulled out a huge wad of bills. "There's the cops, pops. There in my hand. There is the backbone of the cops."

The bartender looked at the money, then at Tony. He licked his lips again, moved his feet nervously.

"Oh, hell," Tony said. "Take out what I owe you and I'll blow this trap."

The bartender pulled a twenty-dollar bill from the mass of money. Tony shoved the rest into his pocket and started to leave.

"Hey," the bartender said. "You got some change."

"Frig the change," Tony said. "Frig you. Frig the world." He went out.

Hell he might as well go to the hotel. He hadn't been back to the bookstore. He didn't want to see Betty again; he didn't know why. June could wait; let her get steamed up enough and maybe she'd hear somebody blow Taps and bust wide open. But Ruthie was back at the hotel. At least there was a drink, too.

Ruthie. Tony hadn't sent any new flesh to Frisco yet. There was something to relieve the boredom. He'd send little Ruthie to a whorehouse. Bye-bye, Ruthie. He walked faster.

Ruthie left the next day. Tony kissed her goodbye and put her on the bus.

Chapter Thirteen

Saturday night. In San Francisco, Tony knew, the clubs would be filled with well-dressed men and women out on the town, drinking and dancing and laughing, listening to the best bands, enjoying the best food and liquor, touching knees under tables, stealing caresses. Cabs would screech around corners, horns would honk, and the clang of street-cars, cable cars, maybe burglar alarms, would be mixing with the scuff of feet on sidewalks and the bubble of sound spilling from the open doors of bars and lounges and cafes. There'd be noise, *noise*, movement, color, life and living, men and women. The San Francisco women, the proud, wise, lovely, soft-fleshed San Francisco women, with their dark-skinned, somber, hard-eyed men.

In Napa there was a street dance.

At six o'clock in the evening, there was no noise except for an occasional automobile, no babel of sound. This was the coffin six feet deep in the graveyard, and the lid was stuck. Tony was kicking the lid off tomorrow, though, heading down the road for somewhere, anywhere but here. The dance was to start at seven P.M. and it was going to be his last adventure in the Napa jungle. He'd seen Ruthie off in the afternoon, talked to a few other women he'd met in the last four days. Ruthie was his only "shipment" so far, but he wasn't in any great hurry about that end yet. There was plenty of time. Too damn much time. That bastard Angelo was the reason for all this; he'd sent Tony out on the job that backfired. An easy guy to hate, Angelo. He sat up in that office of his and took all the gravy, while guys like Tony did the work. It was like way back when he'd done those jobs for Swan; Tony did the job, Swan got the money and credit.

The street dance was held near the center of town, the block roped off at each end. When Tony got there at quarter to seven, there was already quite a crowd present. He hadn't thought there were this many people in town. Not live people. A raised platform on the sidewalk was set up for the orchestra, which wasn't yet present. Tony walked through the crowd, looking around him. There were a lot of young gals and guys, and some old ducks. He saw the slim girl he'd danced with at Hall's Hall, and stopped and talked with her for a minute, then moved on.

Knowing this was his last night here made him feel a little better. At least tomorrow he'd be on his way to some other place; maybe Fresno, Sacramento, he might even buzz clear down to L.A. and Hollywood. Hollywood should be a good spot for him to work in. Anyplace inside the state was O.K. Angelo had warned him not to cross the state line.

When the music started, Tony asked a busty gal about twenty to dance. She was a little heavy, but comfortable to dance with. At first he didn't talk much, but after fifteen minutes, and dances with three different girls, he found he wasn't depressed any longer, was even beginning to enjoy himself. About a quarter to eight, just as another set was starting, he spotted June. He walked up beside her.

"Hi, honey. How about a dance?"

"Well, hi, Tony, sure. I was looking around for you. You been here all the time?"

"Yeah. Since before this wild affair started."

She brushed her blonde hair with one hand, then moved into his arms, close against him. "Isn't this music dismal, Tony? Doesn't do a thing to me."

"Maybe it's a good thing, here on the street." He grinned.

"We get together in the oddest places, don't we?"

"Uh-huh. Always crowded."

She smiled broadly. "Maybe we can find a quieter place some time."

"You know it. Only it better be fast. I'm kissing this dump goodbye." He pulled her closer to him. "Say, your chum around?"

"What chum?"

"Betty. The iceberg."

"Yes. We came down together. She's dancing somewhere."

"You two are a funny pair, June. I mean she's so distant and kind of held back, and you vibrate. I mean you're really a hot number."

"What's so funny about it? We don't sleep together. Besides, we don't go around much, just once in a while. What you always asking about her for?"

"Just talking." They danced quietly for a minute, then she said, "Tony, what did you mean? Are you leaving town?"

"Yeah."

"Why? How soon?"

"Tomorrow. Sooner the better." He paused, squinted at her, then said slowly, "You're still working for twenty a week, huh? Maybe by the time you're fifty you'll be able to save a couple hundred bucks."

She looked at him, running her tongue over her upper lip. "Tony, tell me more about these...friends of yours. These billionaires."

He squinted at her for a half second, then said, "They're salesgirls, honey. They sell meat. Flesh, to be more specific." He kept watching her face. "They sell little hot pieces of flesh, and there's no ceiling on the price." She licked her lips, looked straight back into his eyes, and he went on, "You'd be surprised how few vegetarians there are in San Francisco. A good salesgirl can make a small fortune in a few months or a year—if she handles it right."

She didn't say anything. The dance ended and she

slid up against him as the music stopped, rolled her loins back and forth against his.

Tony said, "Let's dance the next one, O.K.?"

"Wouldn't miss it." She paused. "Salesgirls, huh?"

"Yeah. You know, take a gal making, say, a double sawbuck a week. That's about a thousand a year. Some of these girls I know make that much in a week." That was true enough, but it had happened very seldom, and they were special cases. Tony saw no need to elaborate further, however. The music started and they began dancing again.

Halfway through the fox-trot Tony saw a girl near him, dancing, her back to him. But he knew from the long black hair and the slim waist, the shapely legs under the skirt of her green dress, that it was Betty. She didn't see him, but when the dance ended Tony grabbed June's arm and walked with her to the sidewalk near where Betty stood talking to the guy she'd been dancing with, and another girl. When the guy walked away Tony thanked June and said, "Save me twenty or thirty later. I got something to talk to you about."

"Salesgirls?"

"Yeah, honey."

"O.K., Tony. And…don't forget."

He walked over to Betty. "Hello, there," he said.

She looked around. "Oh. Tony. How are you?"

"O.K. You notice something?"

"What?"

"I didn't call you honey."

She smiled. "I'll bet it was an effort. What are you doing here? You just don't seem the type to be at a street dance, Tony."

"Who, me? I'm crazy about street dances. Say, this is living."

She shook her head and laughed softly. The other girl went off to dance with somebody and Tony and Betty were alone in the crowd.

Tony said, "You mind dancing this one with me?"

She hesitated. "I…don't know."

"Look, dammit, what's the matter with me? I got halitosis or something repulsive? You dance with other guys. I don't get it. Why wouldn't you dance with me last time? You'd think I was asking you to do a trapeze act."

She blinked solemn blue eyes at him. "I—at Hall's, I just didn't feel like dancing, Tony. And I'd seen you dancing with other girls, the way you do."

"The way *I* do? I don't dance different than anybody else."

"Don't you?"

"Well, not different than most guys."

"Anyway, when you asked me, it was—well, like you already knew I'd dance with you. Like you were doing me a big favor. You seemed so sure of yourself, so confident—and conceited—I just didn't want to dance with you."

"For Christ's sake, woman, it wasn't like that at all. Jesus—"

She interrupted. "Tony, do you *have* to talk like that?"

"Look, Betty, I got only one way to talk. I'm me. I talk like me, Tony Romero. How—" He stopped, gritting his teeth. This was the first time he'd told anybody here his full name. He hadn't meant to now; it had just slipped out. But Betty didn't seem to think anything of it so he went on. "O.K. I'll wash my mouth with Fab. Now, let's dance."

She shrugged. "All right, Tony."

He felt silly, arguing with a dame over a dance. That's what getting stuck out in the sticks did to a guy. Here he was hanging around a plain little doll with his tongue hanging out. They walked into the street and Tony put his arm around Betty's small waist, pulled her gently to him as they started to dance. She felt good close to him, her dark hair tickling his chin, the clean smell of her in his nostrils. Strangely, he found himself becoming excited by her nearness, the feel of her brushing lightly against him. Unconsciously, thinking of her wide, full mouth and her white skin, he pulled her closer to him, held her tight.

She pulled away, looked up at him. "Tony…don't hold me so close. Please."

He looked at her, seeing her flushed face, moist, parted lips. She seemed excited, as if she were feeling the same things he was. He looked at her mouth, wanting to kiss it, pull her tight against him and kiss her lips and throat. Jesus, what was the matter with him? A dame was a dame and he could take them or leave them. As he looked at her the music ended and it was suddenly quieter.

"Well," he said, "that was a short one. Let's dance the next, O.K.?"

She didn't answer right away. Then she said, "I don't think I want to, Tony."

"Look, Betty. I hardly got to know you. And I'm leaving here tomorrow. We can at least have a dance or two, can't we?"

"You're leaving? How come?"

"I got places to go, move around. I'm restless. This dead town gives me the shudders. Anyway, I'm going."

Neither of them said any more then, but when the music started they began dancing. Tony held her close to him, and she didn't pull away. They didn't speak. They danced that number and the next one, silently. Tony looked at her face from time to time; she danced with her eyes closed, breathing through her parted lips. He felt funny, an emptiness in his stomach. He wanted to pull her closer and closer, tight against him, squeeze his strong arms around her and mash her soft body to his.

After another dance he said, "Let's walk a little, Betty. Get away from the noise, talk a little."

"All right."

He took her hand and they walked away from the crowd, down a dimly lighted street. Tony didn't know where they were going, he was just walking, holding her hand. He put his arm around her waist and they walked silently, hips brushing occasionally, still not speaking. They neared Tony's hotel and he remembered his car parked in front, and walked that way. When they reached the Buick he opened the door and Betty got in. He drove out of town, up a winding road thickly bordered with trees, then at a small clearing pulled off the road and parked.

She said, "Why did you bring me up here, Tony?"

He turned toward her. "I just wanted to get away from those others, be alone with you." His heart was thudding in his chest and he couldn't explain it, couldn't understand it. In the darkness he couldn't see her, could only feel her nearness. He moved toward her on the seat, put his arm awkwardly around her shoulders and pulled her toward him. She resisted. "Tony," she said, "please, Tony."

Suddenly she relaxed and he pulled her against him, found her face with his left hand in the darkness and tilted it toward him, bent and found her lips with his. Her lips were sweet, soft and gentle, and her arms hesitantly went around him. He felt his blood rushing in his veins, knew her heartbeat was as rapid and heavy as his own as he pulled her tighter against him pressing his hands against her back. When he released her he could hear her panting breath in the darkness. He was breathing heavily.

She said, "Don't kiss me like that, Tony."

"What's the matter? Don't you like me any?"

He could hardly hear her, her voice was pitched so low. "It's not that, Tony. I—you kind of scare me. There's something about you. I don't know. You're—not nice, Tony. I've never been around anyone like you."

His arms were still around her, their faces close together. He kissed her cheek, the corner of her mouth, heard her sigh softly as his mouth moved over hers.

In the dark he could see only the outline of her body, but he could imagine the pale whiteness of her skin. She said breathlessly, "Don't…Tony, please don't…I'm afraid." He didn't speak, his heart beating wildly. He turned, moved close to her, his body finding her body, his mouth finding her mouth. "Oh, Tony," muffled, breathless, "I'm afraid. Oh, Tony…Oh, Tony…"

Later he kissed her tear-stained cheeks, her salty lips. "Don't cry," he said. "What you crying for?"

"I don't know. Honest, I don't know. I just started to cry, is all. Kiss me, Tony, kiss me."

After a while they sat close together, arms around each other. They talked for almost an hour. She told him about herself; she was eighteen, lived with her mother and stepfather. Her mother was sick a lot. She'd lived in Napa all her life, born here. Little things that shouldn't have been interesting to Tony, but were.

Finally she said, "You know almost everything about me, and I don't know anything except your name. And that you're from San Francisco. What about you, Tony? What do you do? I want to know everything about you."

Tony caressed her bare arm and began talking, telling her little things about himself, unimportant things. Suddenly, almost without knowing it, he was telling her about Sharkey, about starting in the racket, about working his way up to where he was now. She didn't speak while he was talking, and he kept on, almost as if he wanted to spill it all out of himself, tell her about it, about everything. The words poured out of him and he kept speaking, not even knowing why he was saying so much. He told her about Maria, about the houses, Angelo, almost everything except the killing of the policeman. Finally he stopped.

After a full minute of silence he said, "Well? Say something. You must have plenty to say now I yakked my brains out."

"I don't know, Tony. I didn't want to dance with you; didn't want to come up here. I didn't want to…do any of it. But I did. But…how can you take money from that? From prostitutes!"

"Hell, what's wrong with it? Somebody's going to; why not me? It's as good as any other money."

"But it's disgusting."

"I don't get you," he said, a trace of irritation in his tone. "There's nothing disgusting about it. Hell, the girls make good dough; they can always get out if they want to—only they don't want to." He paused, thinking. "Listen," he said, "why don't you blow this stinking burg, Betty? I could get you set up in Frisco where you'd make more dough than all these stiffs in Napa got put together. Christ, you're buried in this graveyard."

She laughed slightly. "Tony, if I thought you were serious, I'd really be mad at you. I know you're not."

"What makes you think I'm not serious?"

"Why, you couldn't be. It sounded like you'd actually want me to work in one of those—those houses! You don't mean that."

"The hell I don't. What'd be wrong with it? You'll never get anyplace in this no-man's land. I could set you up in Frisco so you'd make more dough than you ever saw. And, hell, we could be together a lot—and once you'd been in Frisco awhile, you'd never leave the place."

She didn't answer. He listened to the sounds coming from her and said, "Well, Christ, you aren't crying again, are you? What's wrong with you?"

She finally said, "Tony, you're rotten. You're just rotten. I hate you, Tony. I do. I *hate* you!"

"Betty, don't talk like that." He tried to pull her closer, but she squirmed away from him.

"Don't touch me." Her voice was filled with loathing. "I'd rather be with a leper. I mean it. Don't ever touch me again."

He sat with his hands in his lap, looking at her barely visible outline. She sounded cold and mad. What did he get mixed up with such a dopey gal for in the first place? "Betty," he said.

She interrupted him. "Take me home. Now."

"Look, can't we talk sensible?"

"Now, Tony. Or I'll get out and walk."

"Oh, Christ, what a silly thing to say. You act like a baby."

She opened the car door, started to get out. Tony grabbed her arm and yanked her back into the seat. "O.K., dammit. I'll take you home, and be glad of it."

After leaving Betty, he drove straight to the Plaza Hotel, threw his few personal belongings into his suitcase, paid his bill and left. He glanced at his watch as he started out of town, saw it was not quite eleven P.M. He slowed down, thinking, the bubble of anger and an unfamiliar frustration slowly expanding inside him. He swung around and headed back toward the street dance; they'd be clod-hopping around till midnight.

He parked as close to the crowd as he could, got out and walked among the men and women, eyes searching. The crowd had thinned out a little and he soon spotted June's bright blonde hair in the middle of the dancers. He walked up to her and the guy she was with. Tony tapped the guy on the shoulder and as they stopped dancing he said to June, "I want to talk to you."

The man swallowed, looked at June again. She said, "Go on, Lester. I'll see you later, maybe."

June turned toward Tony and started to speak, but he interrupted her. "How'd you like to be a rich sales-girl in Frisco, kid?"

Her eyes narrowed. "Rich whore you mean?"

"Call it anything you want. But make up your mind fast. I'm taking off in about two minutes. You can come along if you want to."

"That's big of you. Don't rush me."

"Oh, go to hell." He turned and started away but she grabbed his arm.

"Wait a minute; don't get mad, Tony. I thought you were leaving tomorrow."

"I'm leaving now. This dump turns my stomach." He paused, then grinned at her. "You got nothing to keep you buried here; you can send Vi a postcard. The car's half a block away. We'll have us some fun, baby. I'll buy you a clarinet."

She licked her lips. "Where you going?"

"Who cares? You name it and you can have it." His eyes narrowed. "You didn't see your little chum here, did you? Little Ruthie?"

"No. Where is she?"

"Probably in Frisco by now. I fixed her up with— with a nice job. She's smart. Hell, she's sixteen; by the time she's eighteen she'll be wearing mink pants. Maybe she's smarter than you, June."

"Not so fast, Tony." She nibbled on her under lip. "How come...you could fix her up so easy?"

He laughed, really amused. "Christ, I forgot to tell you. In Frisco, baby, I'm the Top. I'm the boss."

"You really want me to go with you?"

"I came back and asked you, didn't I? I don't mean we're going to travel around the rest of our lives—you won't have time, you'll be busy. But we'll have us some fun first, kid. Make up your goddamn mind."

She hesitated. "Where's Betty?"

"Forget Betty. You coming?"

"I'd have to pack something, get my clothes."

"And forget the goddamn clothes. I'll buy you some new ones. Well, come on if you're coming." He turned and started walking toward the car.

He was in the Buick, putting the key in the ignition when June came running through the crowd, opened the door and slipped inside. "Damn you," she said breathlessly. "Damn you. All right, Tony. Let me…let me pick up my records."

"All right," he said. "But make it fast." Hell, remembering how hot she'd been in the booth at Westburns, maybe picking up the records wasn't such a bad idea at that.

Chapter Fourteen

In the next month Tony traveled as far South as Bakersfield, and as far north as Willits. He had only one purpose: to recruit girls for the houses, and that activity at first helped stave off his growing boredom. Then finally, boredom, restlessness, and hunger occupied his mind almost all of his waking hours.

He phoned Angelo each week, reported on his activities and asked when the heat would be off and he could come home. Always the answer was: not yet; maybe soon. Each time the reply angered him more.

June was with him for five days, then he sent her on to see Leo Castiglio; she was by that time completely reconciled to being a "salesgirl," and even looking forward to getting started. But after five days Tony was sick of her, as he had been sick of Ruthie. He and June had driven directly to Sacramento, which she had wanted to visit again; after she left, Tony drove up North, then South again to Fresno, Mendota, Coalinga, Bakersfield.

Tony had never had any trouble meeting girls, but now, concentrating on it as on a business problem, he learned how ridiculously easy it was to get acquainted with a girl he'd never seen before. Well acquainted.

The ones who were aloof or distant, he ignored there-
after; the hell with them, there were a hundred eager
babes for each of the cool ones. And the eagerness of
many was accentuated by the big roll of bills Tony
always carried, and by his car. He traded in the Buick
for a new Cadillac convertible sedan, a maroon job
with leather upholstery and white sidewall tires. There
were two girls with him when he traded in the Buick,
paid the rest of the price in cash, and drove out with
them. One of them was on the way to San Francisco
shortly afterwards. She wanted a Cadillac with white
sidewall tires. She never got it.

Tony perfected his approach, his line, his tech-
nique, and the kiss-off when it was necessary. Some of
the girls were easy, some tough, some he got drunk,
some he seduced—and occasionally it was as if he,
himself, were the one seduced—some he just talked
to, put it up to them cold and let them take it or leave
it. Most of them left it, but some got on a bus or train
carrying Leo Castiglio's name and business address
written on a card in their possession. There was no
special "type" most easily recruited, but Tony learned
to look for the young girls who wore much imitation
jewelry, necklaces and bracelets and rings and span-
gles, cheap clothes too tight across their hips and over
their breasts, recklessly applied makeup; he looked for
the inveterate readers of movie magazines and love
stories. He looked for the "easy" girls always known to

a certain segment of a town's young manhood; he looked for the bold eye, the easy smile, the undisguised invitation. But, as the days became weeks, he learned most often to look for the unhappy, the unloved, the rejected, the frustrated.

The first question he asked, casually, of the girls when an opportunity was offered, was about their homes, their parents. Those who were unhappy at home, kicked around, unloved and often unwanted, were his easiest recruits—and there were many of these. They were fairly easy for Tony to recognize, because he had come from the same kind of home. If they were also very poor, there was little for Tony to do except guide the conversations and paint glowing pictures of Cadillacs and fine clothes, bright lights and glittering opportunities. Often he told little but the truth, though when it was in his opinion necessary, he lied easily and glibly—and convincingly. If he had thought about it, he might have found it pathetic that when he told a plain little girl with a fair figure that she looked like Lana Turner or Ava Gardner, she might answer, "I been told it before; only it was Ingrud Boigman. You rilly think so?" But Tony never thought about it.

What Tony thought about was San Francisco—and Betty; the two now seemed to be woven together. Even after those first three days in Napa he had longed for his home, but now there was a hunger in his bowels, a want and a need and a craving for San Francisco. For its crisp, brittle air cold against his cheek, the good wet smell of the fog, the sound of foghorns and ships, the smell and sight of Fisherman's Wharf. He hungered for the crowded, busy streets and the sight of smart, sleek women walking briskly on Geary or O'Farrell or Powell. God, just to walk down Turk Street, if nothing else, past the foul-smelling, dingy dives where the ex-cons and boosters and cannons hang out, the cheap, shiftless, small fry of the rackets; see a drunken stumblebum reel out of Casey's with his shirt unbuttoned, his pants unzipped, whiskers jutting from his wrinkled face and his tie pulled into a knot the width of a shoestring, a black tie most likely, stringy and worn and stained with beer and cheap whisky and wine. To see even that again.

Or to walk into the Patent Leather Room with its black leather walls, its orchids, its soft sweet smell and hum of muted conversation. Then to Bimbo's for a drink and a look at the tiny nude swimmer in the fish bowl, on to the Leopard Room for a steak, maybe even out to the old Barbary Coast, the tourist-trap International Settlement, to get clipped and love it. Or to walk up Grant Street in the heart of Chinatown, stop in Wong's for sweet-and-sour spareribs with fried rice and barbecued pork. Hit the little spots: the Burma Bar to say hello to that fine guy, Harry; the Cable Car Village on California Street to soak up the

Afro-Cuban music, wink at Lynette, shake hands with Russ and Sammy; minestrone on O'Farrell, seafood in Bernstein's.

It was a true hunger, a craving and longing, a hunger in his bowels. And there was with it a hunger in his heart, that was growing into a need, for Betty. Always when he thought of San Francisco he thought of being there with her, walking the streets with her, laughing, drinking, eating, talking, sleeping, loving with her.

Once in a while Tony thought of Maria Casino. But only once in a while. When he did think of her it was with irritation; he forgot or ignored the sweetness of her nature, the pleasant, bright things about her, and remembered the things she did which angered or irritated him.

The combination of his thoughts of Betty and San Francisco, and his studied, humorless conquest and recruiting of the girls, began working a change in Tony. And, too, he had come to loathe what he was doing, not from moral scruples, but from boredom and disgust. His contempt for the "pigs" grew until he sometimes had to force himself to speak quietly and pleasantly instead of smashing his fist into the painted mouth of the girl smiling fatuously at him. Hate grew in him, and grew into his face.

A month and a half after Tony had killed the cop, he ran into a man he had known in San Francisco.

In Sacramento he went into a small, damp-smelling bar for a drink. He recognized his acquaintance immediately, a middle-aged guy named Willie Fife that Tony had seen around and talked to a little. Fife was on the fringes of the rackets, a hanger-on, and a stoolie and informer. Tony didn't have much use for the guy because he figured he'd sell his grandmother for a buck. Tony figured if a guy was going to sell his grandmother, he could get at least a C-note. All the same, Tony was pleased to see a familiar face, and he felt an eager anticipation at the thought of perhaps hearing the latest news from San Francisco.

"Hello, Willie. I'll buy a drink."

The other looked around, surprised at first, then he grinned. "Romero! What the hell you doing down here, man? I thought you were up North."

"I haven't been in Frisco for a month and a half."

"I know you ain't been in Frisco. I thought you was in Oregon or someplace. What's with you, man?"

Willie was short and fat and bald. He had only a small ring of wispy hairs in a half circle on his head, and talked about his receding scalpline but was embarrassed about it. He had a pale, pleasant face with a big crooked nose. He smiled at Tony and said, "Well, buy that drink, man. Bourbon."

Tony ordered two drinks, then moved with Fife to a booth. He said, "How long since you were in town, Willie?"

Willie chewed on his lip. He seemed oddly nervous, Tony thought. "Couple days back," Willie said.

"What's going on in town? Didn't know I could miss the place so much."

They talked for five minutes, Tony listening eagerly to the odds and ends of information. He hadn't even looked at a San Francisco newspaper for over a week, because seeing the familiar names and advertisements, stories of familiar places, made him so homesick he could hardly keep himself from heading back.

Finally Tony said, "Whatever happened on this cop kill, Willie? That Jorgensen guy. Cops getting anywhere?"

Willie licked his lips again, rubbed a hand over his bald head. Tony squinted at him. "What's wrong with you?"

"Nothin', Tony. Nothin'. They got the guy. Didn't you hear about it?"

"When was this?"

"Last week."

"What's the story, Willie?" Tony's hand balled into a fist resting on the table. "Give."

"It was this Floyd Bristol—you know, the junkie. Cops got a tip and picked him up. He, uh, give them a confession. No trial yet, but the cops say it's sewed up."

Tony was thinking: Last week? Why in hell hadn't

Angelo told him to come on back when he talked to him last Saturday? Something was screwy.

Willie was saying, "You and me, we been pretty good friends for quite a spell, right, Tony? I mean, we never had no trouble, got along good. You'd appreciate it if I give you a tip?"

"Sure, Willie." Tony took the roll of bills from his pocket, held them clenched in his hand.

"Well, look—don't get hot at me now," Fife said.

Fife was building up to something. Tony didn't like the feel of it. "Don't worry," he said quietly. "What you got to say?"

"Well, now, I don't know nothin' about this Jorgensen push except what I said, see. And you're a lot closer to Angelo than me, you know. But I get some rumbles, me and the boys, they're around and you hear things, you know."

"Get to the point, Willie."

"O.K. Me and some of us guys what know you, figure you might be getting a little raw deal. There's a hell of a lot of pressure on Angelo, heat's really on, on account of something has to do with you. Word is he's gettin' sick of the pressure. And, well, there's a rumble he's about ready to throw you to the wolves."

Tony's lips were pressed together. He leaned forward. "Look, Willie, let's put our cards on the table. This pressure on Angelo—maybe it's about Jorgensen?"

"That's right, Tony. That's it." Willie seemed to get more nervous. He looked at the wadded bills in Tony's hand, then at Tony's face and away. "I'm takin' a hell of a chance, Tony. If it ever got back to Angelo..."

"It won't." Tony yelled, "Hey, bartender. Two more. Shake a leg." He turned back to Fife. "How big a chance you taking, Willie? How big a financial risk is this?"

"Well, a yard, maybe, Tony?"

What Tony had learned already was easily worth a hundred to him. He pulled three hundred-dollar bills from his roll and shoved them across the table to the other man. "There's three C's, pal. Now give me all of it. Spill your guts out."

The drinks came and Tony paid for them. Willie swallowed half of his in two gulps and said, "Thanks, Tony. Thanks—"

"Skip the thanks."

"O.K. Well, I told you about all. I figure you'll be heading back to town, right? Pretty quick?" Tony nodded. "Well," Fife went on, "I just figure you'd want to know so you can watch your step. Might be it's just a blow-up, but it sounds up-and-up. Maybe Angelo just wants to ease you out because the national ghees been lookin' the setup over. Maybe worse, even."

Tony curled his fist around his glass, then swallowed part of his drink. That "maybe worse" could only mean Angelo might be figuring on getting rid of

Tony for good. Plenty must have happened in the last month and a half.

"Is it maybe?" he asked. "Or do you know."

"No, I dunno. It's just there's a fire under him."

"What's this about national guys?"

"Back East apples. They been in town. Might be they're movin' in. I got it off the wire, but might be there's nothin' to it, for sure." He paused, finished his drink, then said, "Ain't you got a girl back in town?"

"Maria? You might say so. Maria Casino."

"That's her. She's uh, been seeing Angelo. Or he's been seein' her. Anyway, they ain't strangers."

Tony's jaw muscles wiggled slightly. "How long's this been going on?"

"Since you left."

Tony looked at Fife, not seeing him. What the hell was coming off? Everything was going crazy. Maria and Angelo? That didn't even make sense. Christ, there was too much of this all at once. His jaw hardened; he had to get back there, see for himself what was happening.

"You got anything else, Willie? I want all of it."

"That's it, man. That's every bit. And, Tony, thanks for the three yards. I can use it."

"Forget it. I'll see you around." Tony got up and left. He sat in his Cad for a minute, wondering if he should head for Frisco and just bust in on Angelo. He was furious, but he made himself cool down and think logically about it. Barging in on Angelo was no good. And, too, it could be that Fife had things screwed up. No, Tony was supposed to call Angelo again tomorrow night; could be the guy would tell him to come back, that all was now O.K. That was the way to work it: phone the guy and report in, and see what Angelo had to tell him. Play it dumb.

Tony felt better immediately. He'd call tomorrow night—and in the meantime he'd be able to run up to Napa. That's what he'd been wanting to do for the last month; might as well admit it. He lit a cigarette, sucked on it, thinking about Betty. That was about all he'd done, think about her, and he couldn't understand it. Hell, he'd only seen her three or four times; only really been with her that once. It didn't make sense. Maria, even, was prettier than Betty. And the way Betty had acted that last night, she probably wouldn't want to see him anyway. But he knew that he had to see her again, had to talk to her, if nothing else he had to look at her again.

He threw away his cigarette and started the car, felt it leap forward beneath him. As he drove, his thoughts were peculiar ones for Tony. He felt that no matter what was waiting for him in San Francisco, he could handle it, lick it, come out on top—if Betty were rooting for him, if she were with him. It was, actually, the first time in his life that he had qualified his belief in himself, and his confidence. Two months before he would have felt that, whatever waited for him, he could handle it alone.

It was a few minutes after five P.M. when he reached Napa. He drove directly to Westburns, parked and got out of the car. He looked at the book-and-record shop for a moment, his throat dry. He walked to the door, opened it.

He heard her before he saw her. "Tony!" He turned his head and saw her running from the back of the shop toward him. His heart began pounding rapidly and his knees felt weak. She ran up to him, then stopped abruptly, stood in front of him as if suddenly shy.

He swallowed. "Hello, Betty."

She didn't say anything.

He looked around; they were alone in the shop. "I've got to talk to you," he said. "When can you leave?"

"I can close up now." She started to say something else, then busied herself with the last-minute things she had to do before leaving. They went to the door and she locked it. Tony led her to the Cadillac, opened the door and helped her in. He walked around and slid under the wheel.

For a while neither of them spoke, and Tony wondered what was wrong with him, why he couldn't get started saying the hundred things he wanted to say. With other girls or women he was glib, never worrying about the right word or phrase.

He said awkwardly, "Betty, I thought a lot about you. Ever since I left here. I didn't know what you thought or anything, whether you even wanted to talk to me again."

"I've thought about you, Tony. I…I've missed you."

"It's funny, huh? We don't even know each other much. But I been thinking about you all the time." He swallowed, grinned. "If I didn't know better, I'd think…" The words trailed off as he looked at her, as their eyes met.

She stared at him, lips moist and slightly parted, breasts rising and falling. "Oh, hell, Betty," he said after a long silence, "I'm crazy about you." The words he had said a hundred times to other women were stiff and clumsy on his tongue.

She kept staring at him, hands folded in her lap, then she looked away. Sunlight still fell on the streets, but few people were in sight. Betty didn't speak, and Tony started the car and drove away from the store. She had him stop at her house and she was gone for a minute, then ran back to the car. They drove out of town, aimlessly, talking casually of unimportant things, avoiding any reference to the last time they had been together.

As dusk fell Tony pulled off the road and parked.

They sat quietly until Betty said, "Why did you have to come back, Tony? I almost wish you hadn't."

"You said you'd missed me."

"I have. That's why I wish you'd stayed away. Now I'll just miss you more."

"You don't have to, Betty. Not if you're with me."

She closed her eyes, leaned her head back on the seat.

He said, "I came back to see you, talk to you. I'm going back to Frisco tomorrow. I want you to go with me."

"You know I can't, Tony. You know I won't."

"You don't have to do anything. Just be with me."

"Tony, I want to be with you. I don't want to keep missing you like I have." She kept her eyes closed, didn't turn toward him. "But you know I can't just leave. I…don't suppose I'll ever leave Napa till I get married. It's silly to think I'd just go away with you."

She stopped. Tony didn't say anything, thinking of what she'd just said. He'd never considered getting married—and he couldn't even think about marriage now. He had too much to do, too far to go in Frisco. And maybe more than just Frisco. He was going to be an important man, a big man, and marriage was too much like a trap. At least he thought of marriage that way. He thought of the married women he'd been with, gone to bed with; he thought of Ginny and the late Al Sharkey. No, marriage wasn't for Tony.

He said, "Betty, look at me."

She opened her eyes, turned toward him. He said, "Why can't you come to Frisco with me? Be with me. Betty, I don't want to be there without you. We could go tomorrow. Tonight even."

She shook her head. "I can't, Tony. You know I can't."

"Don't you want to be with me, Betty? Don't you..." He stopped.

"Yes, Tony. I do want to." Then she was close to him and his arms were around her and he was kissing her face, her cheeks, her lips and throat. She put her hands on his chest and pushed him away. "Tony, don't."

He moved closer to her, pulled her roughly against him.

Late at night he took her home. They didn't say anything when they arrived there. Tony kissed her, then she got out and went into the house. They'd said all they had to say earlier in the evening. Tony knew he was going back to San Francisco by himself. He knew, too, that if he'd asked Betty to marry him, she might gladly have come; he wasn't sure, because he hadn't mentioned marriage, had ignored her hints. Christ, he couldn't get married, didn't want to consider marriage, even with Betty.

He drove away from the house feeling low and

depressed, unhappy. He was tense inside, tied up in knots. She had been sweet, pleasant, passionate, and even a little tearful. But, Tony thought, maybe it would have been better if he hadn't come to Napa again, had gone instead to San Francisco. Coming here hadn't made him feel any better. He felt worse; about Betty, about everything. He drove downtown and found a pay phone in a drugstore, called Angelo's number.

When Angelo answered, Tony said, "This is Romero. What's the situation back there?"

"Romero? You weren't to call me until tomorrow."

"Yeah? Did I break a rule? Well, what about the heat? Has it cooled enough so I can come back where there's a little action? I'm sick of the sticks."

"Another week or two won't hurt you, Tony." Angelo's silken voice was persuasive. "It's still too hot here for you."

Anger flared in Tony. He knew it was dangerous to speak harshly to Angelo, to the Top, but at the moment he didn't care; he hardly considered his words as rash. "Nuts. What about Floyd Bristol? The cops don't want me any more, I'm coming in."

"I'm closer to things here, Tony. And I tell you it will be better if you wait. The man hasn't even been to trial yet."

"And he won't be for months, probably. I can't wait months, Angelo. I'm about to blow my top. I tell you, I'm coming in."

"Indeed. Well, come if you must, Romero. See me as soon as you arrive." Angelo hung up.

Tony replaced the receiver slowly, squinting. Angelo hadn't sounded at all happy. And Angelo wasn't a good man to have griped at you. Tony thought for a moment of Sharkey, and wondered why the hell he'd talked the way he had just now. It was that goddamn Betty, getting him all stirred up, boiling; why the hell had he got messed up with her in the first place?

He went to his Cadillac and headed toward San Francisco, driving recklessly. He should have been excited at the prospect of returning there, but he didn't experience the leaping pleasure he had expected. He kept thinking that every mile took him farther from Betty. And closer to Angelo.

The interview with Angelo when Tony hit town was simple enough. Angelo merely told Tony to take up where he'd left off, and for Christ's sake to stay out of trouble. But Tony could tell the other man was angry, holding in his anger under a surface of cold calm. There was tension between them while they talked, and it stayed with Tony after he left and drove to his apartment. Seeing Angelo again had crystallized the resentment and irritation with him that Tony had felt for nearly two months; he hated him now. He hated him and admitted to himself that he did.

When Tony stepped inside the apartment, Maria ran to him and threw her arms around him. "Tony," she said happily. "Golly, it's good to see you again, honey."

He put his arms around her automatically, feeling a small pleasure at seeing her again, but that was all he felt. He would almost as willingly have come home to an empty apartment.

"What's the matter, Tony?"

"Nothing's the matter. I'm O.K."

"You look tired. God, I've missed you, honey."

"I've missed you, too, Maria."

Suddenly he wanted to be alone; he didn't want to be around Maria now. But he could hardly leave as soon as he got back. "I am a little tired," he said. "Think I'll go to bed."

"It is late."

"Yeah," he said. "How come you're up? You know I was in town?"

"Angelo phoned me, Tony. I was surprised. I figured you'd let me know soon as you got in."

"I…wanted to surprise you." Angelo, he thought, Willie Fife had mentioned something about Angelo and Maria. He'd talk to Maria about that later. Right now he just wanted to go to bed and try to sleep. In bed, he pretended to fall asleep while Maria cuddled against him.

In the morning Maria seemed a bit sullen, and the discontent had grown in Tony. They spoke little over breakfast. Maria said to him, "What's the matter, Tony? Something's wrong, I can tell."

"Everything's fine."

"It's not. I know you pretty well, Tony. You've changed some way."

"We change every day. Like you, Maria. Like you and Angelo."

She stared at him. "What do you mean?"

"Oh, for Christ's sake, you know what I mean. I know you been seeing him. Haven't you?"

She kept staring at him, then said slowly, "Who told you that?"

"What difference does it make? I know it."

For several seconds she was quiet. Then she said, "I won't lie to you, Tony. I've seen him a few times. But I was worried about you. I wanted to know if you were out of trouble, how you were. You didn't bother much about letting me know."

"Don't give me that." Tony's lips curled, the anger and frustration swelling like a bubble in him, making his words harsh. "What's the matter, couldn't you stand a few weeks without it? And of all the slimy characters to pick!"

Maria's voice rose a little. "I told you why I saw him. He's your boss, isn't he? I don't know why I ever worried about you, anyway. And what's wrong with Angelo?"

"I hate his guts, that's what's wrong with him," Tony said explosively. "So keep the hell away from the bastard."

"I'll do as I please!" Maria stood up suddenly and looked down at Tony, hands on her hips. "You been out of town pawing all the fresh stuff you could get your hands on. I'm supposed to sew it up? You think I'm just supposed to sit here in this dead apartment and write your name over and over or something? You wouldn't even write me, wouldn't even phone me. I suppose you were having too much fun—"

"Shut up!" Tony shouted. "Don't yell at me. You cheap bitch, you stay away from that little bastard. You got to mess with him, you can get your stuff and clear out of here, understand? You can get lost for good."

Maria glared at him, anger coloring her face. Then, suddenly, her features softened. She sat down again and reached across the table to touch his hand. "Tony, what we fighting for? Don't fight with me. I love you, Tony, you know it. Honey, I was with a hundred guys before and it didn't bother you. Why let something like this get you. It don't mean anything. Please, Tony, let's not fight."

"Aw, get the hell away from me."

She bit her lips, eyes narrowing. She said slowly, "What happened while you were gone? You meet somebody, maybe, somebody you like better than me?"

"For Christ's sake what gave you that idea?"

"That's what it is, isn't it, Tony?"

"I met a lot of people. Now knock it off."

"No. If you did, Tony, I *will* get out. You can do anything you want to, but you've got to be mine. If you're not, I'll pack up and go. Maybe that's what you want me to do."

He leaned forward. "Listen, I told you to shut your face. You talk like an idiot. You gonna knock it off or am I gonna have to slap some sense into you?"

She said angrily, "I told you once, Tony, don't ever hit me anymore. You got no more respect for me than to want to slap me around, then I don't want to be with you."

He sighed and got up. "Well, shut up. Let's quit yelling at each other."

She started to reply quickly, then stopped herself and said a moment later, "All right, Tony. I told you I didn't want to fight with you in the first place."

He went out. He headed for a bar and bought a drink, thinking that he was back only one night and he could hardly stand being around Maria. But there wasn't anybody else close to him except her. They'd been together a long time. Christ, what was the matter with him? Why couldn't things stay like they were? He thought about Betty, remembering little things about her, the way she'd smile, the way she'd cock her head on one side and purse her lips when she was seriously considering a question. He had another drink.

Tony drifted through the next days, angered by trifles, irritated with almost everything and everyone about him. He paid little attention to business. And all the time he thought of Betty. He hated his preoccupation with her memory, but it was like an obsession now and he could not stop thinking about her. He wondered, in almost all of his actions, what Betty would think of what he was doing. He had never before in his life had any standard, or moral yardstick, except his own, but now it was as though Betty's words and talks with him, her ideas and beliefs, the things that had shocked or perplexed her, were important to Tony. It was as if Betty, herself, had become a kind of standard by which Tony measured all his actions.

And he finally admitted to himself that he was in love with her. He had been in San Francisco for several days, going through the old routine mechanically, alternating between periods of boredom and anger, thinking of Betty with a kind of sickness inside him. He wanted her with him, wanted her and hungered for her. And he knew that he would have to see her again, at least once again, to tell her how he felt.

He left San Francisco in the middle of the afternoon. He knew he wasn't being smart, wasn't using his head now, but it was something he had to do. He felt that if he waited any longer he'd blow up, start slugging people, do something crazy. He had to get it settled one way or another with Betty before he could think about his job, or even about his life. He didn't tell anybody he was going, he just left, leaving undone the things he was supposed to do.

*

Tony and Betty were alone in the living room of her house; her parents were out. They had gone directly to her home from the store where she worked, and now they were alone together, Tony didn't know how to start. It was the same as when he had last been in Napa. He had felt weak and excited when he saw her again, glad to see her and be with her, but unable immediately to say the right words, tell her what he wanted to tell her.

Finally he said, "I can't seem to stay away from you, Betty. I kept thinking about you every minute."

She said, "Tony, each time you've gone, I've hoped you'd stay away from me. But I think I'd die if you did."

He turned toward her on the couch, took both her hands in his and looked at her. He let his eyes rest on her dark eyes and fair skin, the full red lips. Looking at her mouth he said, "Betty, I told you last time I was crazy about you. But it's even more than that. Worse, or better. I'm in love with you. I been going crazy in Frisco without seeing you. I—Betty, I want to marry you."

Her hands tightened on his, but she didn't say anything.

"Well?" he said rapidly. "I want to marry you. Didn't you hear me?"

"Yes, Tony. But…" She didn't finish.

"But what? Don't you want to get married?" He licked his lips, feeling flushed and feverish, a nervousness in his stomach. "Will you marry me, Betty?"

She hesitated and he felt the nervousness increasing, his throat getting drier. He had expected no hesitation from Betty, had considered only his own feelings and made up his mind that he would marry her. He felt suddenly panicky, then realized that he was squeezing her hands tightly, hurting her, and forced himself to relax.

She said softly, "Tony, I love you. I want to marry you. But...I couldn't be married to you—I don't know how to say it." She paused, then said quickly, "You'd have to do something else, some other work. You know how I feel about what you do."

"What's the matter with it? Look, we just don't think the same way about some things, Betty. There's nothing wrong with it. You'll see."

She shook her head.

He went on, speaking the words in a rush, "I don't make anybody do anything they don't want to do. I just run things. I got a pretty big spot—and I'll get bigger ones. I make enough money so you can have anything you want." He took a deep breath, let it out. "Anyway, you're going to marry me."

"No, Tony. I will if you'll...get out. Do something else. Get a job like normal people and—"

"For Christ's sake," he said, a trace of anger in his

voice. "You want me to be a lousy working stiff, go down to the office at five o'clock every morning, pick up my fifty bucks a week? Betty, what the hell would I do? Sell greeting cards? Wash dishes? Shine shoes maybe? You know I can't do anything like that; I'm on my way now, just getting started. I'm going to be big, honey, really big. We'll be rich. Only I want it with you."

"Tony, you don't understand. I couldn't be married to you when you—when you make money from prostitutes, from something filthy like that."

"Filthy! Are you nuts? Listen, dammit. You know I can't quit. Why the hell don't you grow up?"

"Don't talk like that, Tony. I love you, but I don't like what you do. I couldn't stand it."

He stared at her for a second, jaw muscles bulging, eyes squinting. "Betty, do you want to marry me?"

"Yes, Tony, if—"

"No ifs. I mean right now. The way I am. The way you are. I mean just get married with no prissy, stupid goddamn simpering about what's good or bad or filthy or normal. Right now."

"I couldn't, Tony, I—"

He stood up suddenly, face flushing. "Crap. You don't want a man, Betty. You'd like to marry a hunk of clay; something you could squeeze around any way you'd like it. You get different ideas tomorrow, and you'd want to squeeze it another way. You want something that's got no mind and no bowels." He stood up with his fists clenched at his sides, looking down at her, knowing in his brain that he couldn't have his own life and have Betty, too—and that he couldn't change himself now, even for her. And the hurt and anger grew inside him because he loved her.

"Tony, don't be angry," she said.

"Don't be angry," he mimicked. "What you want me to do? Handsprings? I ask you to marry me, but I'm not good enough for you, no, I'm a slimy bastard. I've probably contaminated the hell out of Napa just by sitting here. Betty, you make me sick."

"Tony! Please, you don't know what—"

"I know I wasted a lot of time messing around with you. Good God, you got no idea there's anything in the world besides this stinking dead town. You belong in a convent where you could play with yourself and think beautiful thoughts. Or a museum."

"Tony. Stop it! I won't have you talk like that."

"You won't? Well, what the hell are you going to do about it? You want me to say, come with me and I'll join the Salvation Army and save happy sinners? I'll study the Bible every night and we can sleep in separate beds—separate rooms. Hell, separate houses. Well, baby, I'm gonna beat it, and this time you don't have to worry about me coming back."

She got up and walked to him and put her hands on his shoulders. "Tony, can't you understand? Can't you even try to see what I mean, see my point of view? I couldn't possibly live the rest of my life with a man who—"

"Drop it," he said harshly. "Don't give me no sermon. Listen, honey, you're all mixed up. You're such a cold-looking piece I figured you'd be terrific once you melted a little. I was right; you're sensational. You'd have made me a mint in one of my houses."

She dropped her hands and stepped away from him, her face getting white. He saw the sudden pain in her eyes, the tightening of the lines around her mouth, and because she had hurt and angered him he went on, perversely wanting to hurt her more. And, too, he knew somehow that he had to separate himself from her cleanly and irrevocably, once and for all, or else continue moving through his life as he had for these last confused and unbearable days.

He stared into her face and said slowly, "That shock you, baby? It shouldn't. I never made no bones about what I am. I'm a king-size pimp, sweetheart, an honest-to-God flesh peddler, and I thought I might be able to do something with you. I already sent a couple of your little friends to my whorehouses—Ruthie and June. You must have missed them. But you're hopeless. I'm slow, but I finally figured it out. So this is the end of the campaign." He stopped, raked his eyes down her body and up it again. "But I could sure have done things for you, baby. Twenty more like you and I could retire."

Her lips were pressed together in a scarlet line across the dead white of her face. She drew back her hand and swung it toward his cheek with all her strength, but he caught her wrist and held it. She stared at him with her eyes wide and her breath racing through her partly open mouth.

He looked down at her for long seconds, not speaking, knowing he was looking at her for the last time, then he let go of her wrist, turned and left the house.

Tony turned the key in the lock, and went inside his apartment, hardly knowing why he had come back to it. He felt as if part of him were dead; he had the crazy thought in his mind that something inside him had died and was rotting and soon the stench would rise to his throat and nostrils and sicken him. He saw Maria walking toward him. There was somebody sitting on the cream-colored couch beyond her: Angelo.

Tony shook his head. There were too many thoughts swirling in his brain. Maria said something to him, but he ignored her words, looking past her to Angelo.

"What are you doing here?" he asked coldly.

Angelo stood up. "Where the hell have you been, Romero? It's after midnight."

"So it's after midnight. So what? I asked you what you're doing here."

"Isn't it obvious, Romero? I've been trying to find

you. You'll get in trouble like this. And watch the way you talk to me."

Tony looked from Angelo to Maria, back at Angelo's face. They both appeared a bit disheveled. Tony grinned tightly. "Sure," he said. "And it's obvious enough. Don't know why I asked. Am I talking all right now?"

Angelo's face hardened. "I want to see you later, Romero. Get over to my office in half an hour."

"Sure. And you can beat it, Angelo."

Angelo frowned, staring at Tony. "What? What did you say?"

"Blow. Get lost." Tony laughed. "You know, beat it."

Angelo seemed not to comprehend for a moment, then the corners of his mouth pulled down. He stared at Tony for a moment longer before he walked to the door, jerked it open and went out slamming the door behind him.

Tony turned to Maria. "I told you I didn't want that bastard here."

"Haven't you got any sense, Tony? Talking to him like that? He wanted to see you."

"Sure. Your face is messed up, honey. Your makeup's smeared. How do you keep from throwing up around that guy?"

"Will you listen to me? He came here looking for you. I told you a while back there was talk about the Eastern bunch coming in here. Well, Angelo's got something on the fire. That's why he was so anxious to see you."

Tony remembered Willie Fife saying something about the Syndicate coming in; there'd been some noise about that for quite a while now, and maybe things were coming to a head.

He said, "What about the Syndicate bunch?"

"I don't know. He'll tell you. But there's something supposed to be settled tonight. It you'd been here there'd of been no trouble. But Angelo's going to talk to them tonight."

"He couldn't send one of his boys here, could he? He had to come himself? You have fun, baby?"

"You're a fine one, Tony. Don't you think I can figure out where you went? The way you been acting lately, it's easy to figure. You went to see that girl, who-ever she is."

"Betty, honey. Not 'that girl.' " He laughed again. "We're a great pair. I'm out talking to a girl half in the cradle, and you're in bed with Angelo."

"I wasn't in bed with him."

He shrugged. "So you missed tonight."

"You wouldn't care if I went to bed with a horse. Tony, I don't know, I just don't know. You're not Tony Romero any more. You're not you. And I don't like the way you are."

"I like it. Now shut your face." He went to the bar and began mixing a drink. Maria walked up to him.

"Tony, listen. I told you a long time ago you were getting in too deep, and if you kept on you wouldn't be able to get out. Now the Syndicate's coming in. Maybe that'll be bad for you, I don't know. But you've got to slow down. And the way you talked to Angelo—you can't do that, Tony. You got to take it easy, especially if the big guys come in."

"I told you to shut up. I'm doing O.K.—and I'll do better. Angelo doesn't bother me a bit."

"He'll probably talk to the Syndicate men tonight. Doesn't that bother you? You can't get funny with them."

"So maybe I'll talk to them, too. Angelo's not the only guy can talk to them, is he? Maybe I'll talk to them instead."

She frowned at him. "What do you mean? Don't talk crazy, Tony. What's the matter with you? You going crazy or something? You talk like you're out of your mind. You've already gone too far with Angelo."

Tony swallowed at his drink, ignoring Maria. She griped him, always worrying, yakking at him about something. It was like having a nagging wife.

She said, "Tony, you could still get out. We could go somewhere away from here and—"

He turned to her angrily, "Stop this get-out crap. I told you before. I'm in and I'm staying in."

She put a hand on his arm, kept talking, pleading with him to get out of the racket while he was still all right, still alive. Rage built in him as he glared at her, watched her mouth working. This was the same kind of thing Betty had given him, the same, stupid woman argument, trying to change him, make him something that he wasn't. He stared at Maria's mouth opening and closing, only half hearing her words, rage growing and burning, flaring hotter.

"I tried to tell you," she was saying. "But you act like you're crazy, like you're—"

He swung the back of his closed fist against her mouth. She staggered, and fell to the floor, blood starting to spill from her lips. He walked to her and stood over her. "I told you to shut up!" he said loudly. "I told you to quit yapping at me. Now will you stay shut up?"

She put a hand to her mouth and rubbed it over her lips, never taking her staring eyes from him. Slowly she got to her feet. "That ends it," she said. "That ends it, Tony. I'm getting out."

"Good. Beat it. Maybe you can catch Angelo. The sonofabitch. I ought to fix him a little, too. Maybe I will."

She turned away from him and went to the closet, started taking clothes from hangers. Tony walked up beside her. "If you're getting out, get out now," he said. "Just the way you are, baby. Go on, beat it."

She dropped the clothes to the carpet, walked stiffly to the door and outside. Tony went to the bar and tossed down his drink. Then he threw the glass across the room, shattering it against the wall, and put his head in his hands, squeezed it. He swore violently, then raised his head and looked around him like a man dazed.

Everything was going to hell, everything. And he was still supposed to see Angelo, some goddamn thing about the goddamn Syndicate. He went to the bedroom and got his gun harness and Magnum, strapped them on. He mixed a short one at the bar, drank it, and went out.

Chapter Fifteen

Angelo clipped the end off a cigar and stuck it into his puckered mouth. He looked up at Tony, then struck a match and held it to the cigar's end. Between puffs he said, "We can't afford to bicker with each other, Tony. I realize a man's nerves get on edge sometimes, but that's to be expected." He took the cigar from his mouth, looked at it.

Tony glanced across the room. Frame and Rock sat in two chairs against the wall, Frame with one leg looped over the chair arm, heavy Rock slumped down with his legs stretched out in front of him. There were only those two others in the room.

Angelo glanced up at Tony. "Sit down," he said.

Tony sat in his usual chair and waited for the other man to go on. Angelo seemed pleasant enough, didn't appear to be carrying a grudge because of the way Tony had talked to him at the apartment. Tony felt a little relief ooze through him at the thought; he'd been so keyed up and angry and confused that he'd spoken recklessly to Angelo, but maybe no harm was done.

Angelo said, "You're the number-one man under me, Tony. We simply can't afford to bicker or have any difficulties between us. Don't you agree?"

"Sure. I been having a couple little troubles, Angelo. But that's all taken care of now."

"I'm glad to hear it. I know you've been under a strain, Tony. There's very little that escapes my attention." Tony thought the guy's voice was actually syrupy. Almost too soothing and silken. Angelo had done a complete about-face from the way he'd acted at the apartment.

Angelo went on, "There'll be two men here shortly from Chicago, Tony. They're coming into the operation. It will mean changes, but quite a bit of the load will go off our shoulders."

"How do you mean?"

"The operation will be expanded even further— they have houses stretching clear across the country, so there can be a constant supply of new faces. They'll handle that end. There should be enough more money so that we all do better."

"Including me?"

"Of course, Tony."

"Where do I fit into the new picture?"

"The same as now. But…" Angelo paused briefly, then went on, "…as I said, Tony, you seem to have been under a strain. I think you should take a little rest."

Tony didn't like the way the conversation was going. Something was screwy. He said, "I just had a long vacation—too long. I'm O.K. now."

"Let me be the judge of that, Tony." Angelo's voice was the merest bit harder. "What I had in mind was a different line of activity for you. Do you remember that nightclub you mentioned to me a while back? The one not now in use?"

Tony thought a minute. When he'd been casing locations for the queer house, he'd looked over that nightclub, thinking it could be fixed up into a nice spot with tables below and beds above. It was quite a distance out of the city. "Yeah," he said. "I remember the place."

"I'd like to start it up. Put you in charge of the spot, Tony—not for more than three or four months, you understand. Just till you could get it going. Then, of course, you'd return to running the houses for me. By that time, too, all the details of the collaboration with the others—the Chicago men—will be smoothed out. How does that sound?"

Tony said casually, "It might be all right."

"I'm sure it will be. Frame and Rock here—" Angelo nodded his head—"will work with you, directly under you. I've already spoken to them about it. You three can go out there tonight and look the place over, see what has to be done. I'd like to get it started as soon as possible. Perhaps you could get the painters and carpenters in there tomorrow."

"Sure," Tony said. His lips felt a little numb. Christ, what a sap he was; he'd been long enough figuring out what was up. His heart started beating faster.

Angelo said, "Well, that's about all, Tony. I wanted this started yesterday—but I couldn't find you. Look the place over tonight and report to me in the morning. You'll be in complete charge."

"Swell," Tony said. His brain was like ice. It was obvious now: They were going to kill him. This was a nice, civilized ride, the bump-off of Tony Romero.

He managed to smile pleasantly. "Sounds all right, Angelo. Change'll probably do me good."

Frame and Rock got out of their chairs. Angelo said, "That's all, then. Call me tomorrow."

Tony got up. "Sure, Angelo. I always wanted to sharp up in a tux and watch the tables. Come on, boys, get the lead out."

Rock drove his own car; his shoulder seemed to be O.K. now. Frame sat in the back with Tony. They were halfway to the nightclub. Tony remembered the spot well: a big place, boarded up, no other houses or buildings for blocks, a lot of trees and shrubs around and a driveway veering in from the road and curving in front of the club. It was a good place for what was supposed to happen.

Tony's palms were sweating. Frame had been joking with him, cracking wise and laughing all the way. The atmosphere was one of jovial good fellowship, a lot of laughter, and some smutty stories. Tony had guessed, in Angelo's office, what this two o'clock ride was for, but now the forced hilarity and continual conversation made him positive that he had guessed right. That sonofabitch, Angelo, had finally made up his mind because of the way Tony had talked back at the apartment. Or maybe it was his taking off in the afternoon, dropping everything. Could be, too, that Angelo was simply fed up with Tony, perhaps a little afraid of him, or maybe Tony wasn't needed now that the national Syndicate was coming in. Getting too big for Angelo's taste, maybe.

Tony bit his lip, thinking. There was something else, another good reason: Maria. He'd slugged her around, kicked her out—and she knew about Betty; what she didn't know for sure, she had guessed. And Tony had run off at the mouth to her, saying he could talk to the Chicago boys as well as Angelo, that maybe he'd work Angelo over a bit, too. The bitch might have got in touch with Angelo, called him, told him Tony was getting out of hand, reckless, maybe was thinking of crossing Angelo himself. That would have made up the little bastard's mind for sure; and he seemed hot for Maria, anyway. No telling how thick they'd got in the last month or two, and with Tony planted Angelo would have a clear field. The conviction grew that probably it *had* happened like that.

He stopped thinking about it, tried to keep his mind

on what Frame was saying. He had to get out of this some way. At least his gun was still under his coat; they might take it away from him—or they might simply shoot him in the back. He was holding himself tense; he tried to relax.

Frame said, "We got to go to another of them parties like that one, Tony, boy." He had been talking about a tea party up on Nob Hill before Tony had taken over Alterie's district.

"Sure," Tony said. "I had a hell of a time. Maybe we can have another poker game some night."

Frame and Rock laughed loudly. They laughed loudly with the slightest excuse. "Yeah, man," Frame said. "This club would be a good spot—got everything practically set up there already."

"Hey," Tony said, "we're gonna look the place over; the electricity on out there?"

"Why, sure. How else we gonna see to do the job?" Frame and Rock laughed again.

In another minute Rock turned off the road and went over the rutted driveway. Weeds grew in front of the empty club, barely visible in the moonlight. The car's headlights flashed across the front of the building, showing the faded and peeling paint. The car stopped and Rock turned off the lights. When Rock switched off the engine, Tony could hear the faint sighing of the wind.

"Let's go," Frame said.

Tony hesitated only a moment, then stepped outside the car, holding his right hand close to the butt of the gun. He didn't think they'd start anything yet; probably it was supposed to happen inside the club. The entrance was only a few feet away and Tony followed closely behind Frame as the other headed for it. Behind him Rock slammed the car door and came after them. Tony wrapped his palm around the butt of his revolver and eased it from its holster, the cold wind rippling over his skin. The flesh of his back crawled; Rock might be leveling a gun at him this very second. Frame was close ahead, though. Tony stepped up near him as Frame pulled a key from his pocket and unlocked the door.

"Go on in, Tony; I'll get the lights."

Tony stepped quickly through the doorway into musty darkness. Apparently it was to happen in seconds now—unless Tony had it figured wrong. He walked rapidly ahead through the darkness, waiting for the flash of light. If nothing was supposed to happen, this was still going to be damn fatal for somebody. Tony held the gun solidly in his palm, ready to start shooting as soon as there was light. He stopped and turned, the Magnum pointing toward the doorway, fear crawling in his stomach, his heart racing.

The lights blazed on. He saw Frame standing at the right of the door, one hand on a light switch, the other holding a gun. Rock stood just inside the doorway, an

Army automatic held in front of him, just swinging toward Tony as light filled the room. He was hunched forward slightly, his eyes narrowed.

Tony fired a split second after the lights blazed in the room. He jerked his gun toward Rock, pulling the trigger even before he could aim, kept pulling it as the gun centered on Rock's beefy, squat body. Noise cracked and echoed in the room; Rock staggered. Another gun boomed and a bullet slashed across Tony's cheek as he saw Frame leap from the wall, a yell ripping from his lips.

Everything was blurred, shifting, to Tony, two-dimensional and unreal. His brain seemed calm, but with an icy coldness, as if this wasn't himself at all but a robot going through motions, moving automatically. He saw Rock crumpling as his eyes shifted to Frame, saw the man jumping to the side, the automatic in his hand raised, flame spurting from the muzzle as Tony pulled the Magnum to bear on the moving body and pulled the trigger, pulled it again. Frame staggered, moved forward another two steps, then fell to his knees, toppled to the floor, the gun sliding from his hand.

Rock lay quietly, face down. Frame moved, gasped, kept trying to get up. Tony stared from one to the other, mouth open; barely comprehending that the split moment of surprise had given him enough advantage. It was all over now. At least it was almost over. He checked the Magnum. There were two unused cartridges left in the chambers. He stepped to Frame, grabbed him roughly and jerked him to a sitting position.

"All right, you bastard. Give. How many of you were in on this? What did Angelo tell you?"

A little blood bubbled from Frame's mouth. He shook his head, mumbling. Tony left him for a moment, picked up the automatic, then went over to Rock. Rock was dead. One of Tony's slugs had bored from a spot near his left eye into his brain. Tony walked back to Frame.

"Spill fast."

"Doctor." Frame's eyes were glazed with shock.

"Sure, I'll get you a doctor, Frame. Get you all fixed up—*after* you spill."

Frame's head wobbled. He squeezed his eyes shut, grimacing, then opened them wide. "Just us. Rock 'n me. Angelo said, get rid you. Christ, a doc, Tony. I'm bleedin'. I'm hurt bad."

"Sure. Why the bump-off?" Tony thought again about Maria, the chance that she'd phoned Angelo, said Tony was getting wild ideas. It was hard for him to think; there seemed to he a tingling all through his body, a heady kind of intoxication in him, racing with his blood. "Why, Frame? Quick! Angelo must have told you something."

Frame wobbled his head again, lips slack and looking bloodless, pulled back from his decaying teeth. "Nothin'. I swear it. Oh, Jesus. Just said to do it."

Tony raised the Magnum and pointed it at Frame's forehead. "Don't lie to me, you sonofabitch. Angelo must have said something else. He get a phone call? Anything? What about the Chicago boys? That have anything to do with it?"

"I dunno! I swear I dunno." Frame tried to move his head back away from the barrel of the gun, panic in his eyes. He rolled his head, inched away, fell backward full length, more blood trickling from a corner of his mouth.

"I dunno. Swear it, Tony, please. Oh, God, get me a doc."

Tony believed Frame, believed he didn't know any more than he'd said. "Sure, man," he said. "I'll get you a doc."

He stepped closer to Frame, leaned over the prostrate man and put the gun against his forehead. For just a moment Frame realized what was going to happen and his eyes stretched enormously wide. But it was for only a moment.

As the gun blasted, Frame's body jerked once, and slowly relaxed and lay still. The room was awesomely quiet, then, but Tony could hear his heart drumming, booming in his ears. He felt as if he were floating, as if his body were as light as air. He looked at Frame, at the awkwardly hanging, red-stained mouth.

His mind flashed crazily back over the months and years, to Sharkey's dead face, to the first time he'd seen Sharkey, his drunken mouth hanging open later that night much as Frame's dead one did now. Christ, it had been easy to kill Frame, he thought. It had all been easy. He remembered the poker party, Sharkey murdered with Tony's gun; then Tony had killed that bastard cop in self-defense. Then Rock, just a moment ago—that was a case of kill Rock or be killed himself, too, but Frame had been something else entirely. He'd killed him because he wanted to kill him; a few seconds before it would have been the other way around. Frame would have murdered him in cold blood. He'd got what was coming to him.

Tony stared down at the dead man, feeling nothing except that tingling exhilaration he always felt at times like this, when he was charged up, tense, excited. He wondered for a moment if there were really something different about him, something wrong with him. That time when he'd fought with Alterie, other similar moments when he'd felt strange and good as he felt now, hardly knowing what he was doing. He shrugged, straightened up. His thoughts shifted to Angelo. That was the sonofabitch who'd put out the word: kill Romero. Angelo, always Angelo, always in Tony's hair, always raking in the big gravy while the guys under him did the work—like this, tonight. Tony stared at the wall, not seeing it, his mind racing. He glanced once at Frame and Rock, dropped Frame's automatic into his coat pocket, and went out.

Tony parked Rock's car on Market Street, got out and stared up at the tall building for a moment, then rang for the night watchman, who let him in. The watchman took Tony up to the tenth floor, and went back down in the elevator as Tony walked to the "National Investment Counselors" and paused outside the door. Light seeped out into the hall from beneath the door. Tony breathed heavily through his open mouth, holding the Army automatic in his right hand. He knew Angelo would be in the inner office, but maybe the outer one was empty. And, too, those guys from Chicago might be there now—or they might have come and gone. Tony paused only a moment; this was no time for him to hesitate, he thought; whatever he was going to do would have to be done tonight, now. He wasn't even sure what he would do; it depended on whether or not Angelo was alone, what he said, a lot of things.

He turned the doorknob and a track of light spilled into the hall, widened as the door opened. He could see nobody inside. He went in and looked around. The room was empty, and the plain door leading into Angelo's office was closed. Tony walked soundlessly across the carpet and slowly, carefully tried the knob. The door was locked.

He swallowed, licked his lips and put the automatic in his right coat pocket, hand around the butt, then knocked loudly. He waited. The door swung open and Angelo looked out at him. Tony jerked the gun from his pocket and jabbed it into Angelo's stomach.

"Hold still," he hissed. "Don't move, Angelo." Angelo's mouth dropped open, his face paling. Tony pushed the door wide and glanced past Angelo into the office, then shoved the small man backward. Angelo had been alone. Tony slammed the door shut, bolted it.

"Stand right there, you bastard," Tony said. He crossed to the door leading into the adjacent room, turned the bolt, then stepped toward Angelo.

Angelo hadn't spoken. Now he said, "Wait, Tony, what's—what's the matter? Why...what is it, Tony?"

"You sonofabitch, you know what it is. Your kill missed, that's what it is. I came back to report on the club. Needs some alterations. Couple dead bodies got to be moved out. And one out of here, maybe."

Angelo's face was a ghastly white. Tony had never seen him really frightened before; he was frightened now. "I don't know what you mean, Tony. Put...put away that gun." Angelo's eyes flicked from the gun to the door, then to Tony's grim face.

Tony said, "Remember our talk a little while ago? About there shouldn't be difficulties between us? Well,

I know exactly what you meant now. I learn fast—you know that, Angelo. And I want to know your reason for setting up the ride tonight."

"Why, Tony, I don't—"

Tony stepped forward and cracked the automatic across Angelo's cheek. The other fell, sat up shaking his head. "That'll give you an idea I'm serious, Angelo. You might as well tell me before you get more." Tony moved the gun in his fist.

Angelo got to his feet, his face twisted with fear. "It was a misunderstanding, Tony. Believe me." Tony stepped toward the smaller man again and Angelo said hastily, "Wait! Wait, Tony. I...it was the Chicago men."

"You've seen them, huh?"

"No—yes! They did it."

"Stop it, you bastard. One more lie and I'll kill you. I mean it." The automatic was cocked and ready to fire. Tony pointed it at Angelo and tightened his finger slightly on the trigger.

Angelo put both hands out in front of him, backed away. "No, no! It—all right, Tony."

"Have the guys from Chicago showed up yet?"

"No. That's the truth. But they'll be here soon, any minute. Stop and think, Tony. You can't—can't do anything. They'll be here."

"What's the deal with them?"

"It's simple. Just a percentage. They'll supply girls, help run the operation—like a partnership. They'll be here soon, Tony, just to make sure it's all settled."

Tony grinned. "Sounds like nothing to it. I could handle it for you, couldn't I?"

"Yes, Tony. Of course; it's almost settled. I'll let you handle it." Angelo's words were twisted as they spilled from his mouth.

"Sure, you'll let me handle it." Tony was enjoying himself. Enjoying watching Angelo squirm after all the crap Angelo had given him. "Listen, why the bump-off?" Thoughts swirled in Tony's mind again. "Was it Maria?"

"Maria?" Angelo looked puzzled. "How do you mean?"

"Did she give you any song and dance about me?"

"Maria?" Angelo ran his tongue over dry lips. "Why—yes. Yes, Maria said…" His voice trailed off. "Put the gun away, Tony. I can't talk with that gun pointing at me."

Tony stared at Angelo, at the man's small, fear-stained face, feeling the contempt and hatred growing in him. Angelo, the Top, the gravy guy. Tony knew he was going to kill the sonofabitch. Angelo out, Tony Romero in. That's the way it should have been a long time ago. And he couldn't wait much longer. The boys from Chicago might be here any minute; Tony could talk to them, make the deal with them as easily as Angelo. At least they'd soon be here if Angelo were telling the truth. You couldn't tell if the scared little bastard was telling the truth or not. Angelo; the only good Angelo was a dead one. With Angelo dead, Tony would be on top, in the driver's seat. Thoughts jumped and whirled in a jumble in his brain. He stepped toward Angelo, raising the gun higher.

Angelo moved away from him, his mouth wide. He bumped into the wall and pressed against it, turning his head to the side, staring at Tony from the corners of his eyes as if afraid to look directly at him, and at the gun.

"Tony," he said. "Tony. Stop, wait a minute, Tony."

Kill him now, thought Tony. I killed two guys already, I'm in it good now. Kill this bastard before something goes wrong. Let him get out of this and you're dead for sure. Kill him and you're in, *you're* the Top. Kill him, kill him.

The words danced in his brain as Angelo's face seemed to blur before him. Angelo was speaking rapidly, a flood of words that meant nothing. Tony stepped closer, the gun held in front of him. Angelo shrank back against the wall. He screamed, "No, Tony, no—" and thrust his hands up before his face as Tony fired the gun.

The automatic leaped in Tony's fist as the heavy

bullet tore through Angelo's hand, slamming it back against his mouth. Angelo's head thudded against the wall, and the moment afterwards be crumpled to the floor, limp, lifeless.

After the sound of the shot there was noise at the door of the adjoining office. Tony whirled and saw the knob turn. The door was locked, but somebody banged on the door and Tony heard a muffled shout. He walked to Angelo's desk, sat down in the chair behind it. He put the gun on the desk top and wiped his hand on his coat, his mind frozen. He sat there for long seconds, staring at the gun. Well, he'd done it, he finally thought, his brain working sluggishly. Angelo was dead. Christ, just a little squeeze of one finger and Angelo was dead. God, how easy it was. Tony bit his lip. He was in now—but he'd have to work it right. Have to be careful now, not mess it up. He had to convince everybody he was the boss. He glanced at the locked door; somebody was still pounding on it. He forced himself to think. Have to be careful what he said to the Chicago men. That was something. What was he going to say? He shrugged, shook his head. He'd handle that when it happened. And there was Maria, too. Had she put the bug in Angelo's head? He didn't know; but she could have. Probably she had. The bitch, just because he'd slugged her for yakking her fool mouth off. She'd had it coming. Maybe she hadn't said anything to

Angelo, though. Christ, he couldn't think straight. The hell with it. Figure it out later. Got to get rid of Angelo, get him out of here.

Something heavy crashed into the door. Tony got up, lit a cigarette. He had to be the boss now, the Top, himself. He walked to the door and slammed his hand against it twice. The noise on the other side stopped. Tony licked his lips, then shoved the automatic into his coat pocket. He opened the door.

Joyce burst into the room, followed by young Kelly. Joyce stopped. "What the hell's going on?" He started to look around the room, a gun held in his right hand. "Where's the boss? What—"

"I'm the boss. Get that, Joyce, and get it fast." Tony pointed with his left hand, right hand around the gun in his pocket. "There's what was the boss."

Joyce gasped and Kelly swung his head to stare at Tony. Joyce slowly turned his head and Tony snapped, "Get rid of that. Get rid of it good and do it fast."

Joyce hesitated, blinking his pale eyes. This was too sudden for him. Tony knew he had to keep the initiative while he had it; if the men were able to give him trouble now there'd be plenty more later. He stepped closer to Joyce, put a hand on his shoulder and shoved him toward Angelo's body. "Didn't you hear me? Get rid of that. Now!"

Automatically Joyce moved toward the body, Kelly

following. Tony walked behind the desk, sat down where Angelo had always sat. "Take it into the next room; move him out from there. I'll talk to you later."

The men moved numbly, carried the body out. Tony walked to the front door and unbolted it, then sat down behind the desk again. The visitors Angelo had expected should be here soon. He waited, thinking, realizing that he'd meant to kill Angelo all along.

Chapter Sixteen

When the knock came on the door, Tony called, "Come in," took a deep breath and let it out slowly.

Two men stepped inside, both medium-sized, conservatively dressed in dark single-breasted suits. They looked more like prosperous businessmen than anything else. Which, thought Tony, they were.

The first one in, a dark-skinned man with a wide, square chin, walked up to the desk. The other one, slimmer and a little shorter, followed.

Tony said, "Sit down, gentlemen."

The dark-skinned man hesitated. "We were to see Angelo."

"Angelo had...an accident. I can talk for him. I'm Tony Romero."

The man nodded, glanced at the slim guy, then back to Tony, the two men sat down. The first man said, "I'm George Mint. This is Saul Rash." He indicated the slim man.

Tony thought the names would fit them better if they were Minetti and Rashbaum, but he merely nodded. Mint said, "What kind of an accident did Angelo have?"

Tony said quickly, knowing they'd soon learn the

truth, "He got himself killed." He pointed to the bullet hole in the wall and the stain around it. "Just a little while ago." He paused. This was the bad part, no telling what these guys might do. "But," he went on, "there's no reason why that should affect the...business you wanted to talk about. I know everything that goes on in San Francisco. As a matter of fact, I'm the man who actually runs the houses. Angelo had very little to do with that end."

He waited. He waited for quite a while before either of the men spoke. Mint was the one who finally broke the long silence. "I see. Perhaps we can still do business. It would be unfortunate if this forced any changes in our plans. Or delayed things."

"I'm sure it won't. The name's Romero instead of Angelo, that's the only difference." Tony was nervous. There was a lot about this that he didn't know—and, too, although Tony knew almost all of Angelo's channels and contacts in the city government and police force, he didn't have them under his thumb the way Angelo had. But, he thought, that part wouldn't take too long; he'd manage it.

They talked for another fifteen minutes, discussing what had been previously arranged with Angelo, agreeing on the new policy and partnership. It was simple enough. About all that Tony had to do was agree, nod his head, or explain some facet of the business, locations and kind of houses, amount paid for "ice" or protection. With all of that Tony was perhaps even more familiar than Angelo had been.

He thought the men were quite satisfied, but after they got up and were ready to leave, Mint said, "Mr. Romero, all of this sounds satisfactory, but I'm afraid we'll have to postpone our decision. The fact that Angelo is, uh, dead, means we'll have to discuss this with others. I'm sure it will be all right. You don't mind waiting another day, do you?"

"Certainly not."

"Say we meet tomorrow."

Tony nodded.

Mint looked at Rash. Rash, who had taken very little part in the discussion, said, "Pop's?"

Mint nodded and turned to Tony. "What say we meet about two in the afternoon at Papa Sol's? You know where it is?"

"Don't remember it."

"Little Italian spot; good food. Have lunch there and wind this up. All right?"

"Sure." Mint gave Tony the address and directions, then the men left. After they'd gone Tony stood looking at the closed door for a moment. Why the hell they want to meet way out there? It was clear the hell out past Twin Peaks on Junipero Serra Boulevard. He didn't like it. It sounded too much like going out to "look over" that closed-up nightclub. Well, he was in it now; he'd figure something.

He waited till Joyce and Kelly came back, their job finished, told them he was going home and would be down at nine in the morning. Then he left. There was plenty to do tomorrow: make sure there was no stink about Angelo that couldn't be quashed; start seeing some of the late Angelo's contacts; check into the current status of Floyd Bristol, the "cop-killer"; case Papa Sol's and see if he could find out how the wind out there was blowing. There were a million things to take care of, but once things got rolling smoothly he'd really be on his way. He relaxed a little for the first time in hours, feeling weariness tugging at his muscles.

He drove toward his apartment, thinking. If things went well, Tony Romero might be on his way to becoming one of the most important men in the United States, a really big one. He smiled slightly, plans already forming in his head. If he got in with the Syndicate O.K., he might even get a slice of other rackets—maybe the gambling and narcotics. Terrific dough in the narcotics game. He'd have to watch his step from here on in, but with a little luck he'd have it made. A guy like Tony Romero could always get bigger and better spots, more dough, more power. He was still jumpy and keyed up, but he was starting to feel pretty good. If only his luck held—but hell, he thought, a guy made his own luck. He'd known that from the beginning: a guy had to help make his own breaks. He'd made his own, and they'd paid off.

He wondered what Betty would think of him when he got up to the top, one of the really big ones. She might be O.K. when she dried out behind the ears a little. He parked and went up to his apartment, let himself in, still thinking of Betty, feeling something that was nearly hate for her. He stopped inside the door, looking around. Something was different, out of place. For a moment he didn't get it and fear swelled in his throat at the thought that maybe Mint and Rash hadn't gone for his spiel back there, might have planned to get rid of him, take over completely—then he saw what it was that had stopped him inside the doorway. There were clothes draped on the couch, women's clothes, and two suitcases there. He glared at them as Maria came out of the bedroom carrying another traveling bag.

He swung toward her, the remnants of the fear that had been in him combining with the long-drawn-out tenseness of the last few hours.

"What the hell you doing here?" he asked roughly. "I told you to beat it."

She didn't answer. She placed the bag by the others, opened it and stuffed the clothes from the divan into the already half-filled suitcase.

Her silence infuriated him. "Goddammit, answer me."

She rose and faced him. "I came for my things. They're mine." Her lips were puffed out, ugly, and she moved them only slightly as she spoke. "I won't be here long. It makes me sick to be here."

"You bitch," he said. "Maybe you're here because you didn't think I'd be back. Maybe you thought Angelo would be here instead. That right?"

She frowned at him. "I don't know what you mean."

"Yeah, you know what I mean. You thought I wouldn't be able to come back, that I'd be dead. Well, Angelo's dead instead. You sad? I bet that breaks your heart."

She looked at him, eyes narrowing. "Tony, you're rotten. There's no trust in you any more—maybe there never was. You know that anybody's a fool to trust you, so you can't trust anyone yourself." She stopped, then said calmly, "You're rotten, Tony; I hate you. It took you a long while, but you finally made me hate you."

He stepped toward her, anger darkening his features, and grabbed her arm. She jerked away from him, lips twitching. "Don't touch me. I think if you touch me again, ever again, I'll—I'll vomit. You make me sick, Tony."

He stopped close to her, glaring down at her, breathing heavily. Damn her, she was giving him the same stuff again, the same kind of crap Betty had given him that night when she'd run from the car into the house.

"Shut up," he said. "Shut up and get out of here. I got no more use for you."

"No more use for me," she said bitterly. "Or Alterie, or Leo, or Swan—or Angelo now, I guess. You've got no use for people when they can't help you. Well, Tony, I've no use for you. Nobody else has, either. Don't you know that?" She paused. "You haven't a friend in the world. You haven't anybody. Not even me, now." She smiled slightly, twisting her bruised lips. "How about your girl? Your Betty? Where's she, Tony?"

"Shut up. I'm warning you—"

She laughed shrilly. "Everybody hates you, Tony. I hate you. I think you hate yourself. And how about your Betty—"

Tony's teeth were pressed together until his jaws ached. Why didn't she shut up? She was driving him nuts with her yakking. He shouted at her, but she kept on, taunting him.

"All right, you bitch," he said violently. He swung his fist up from his hip, felt it jar against the side of her face, felt a strange, savage pleasure course through him as his fist struck her flesh and she reeled away from him, stumbled and fell. He stepped toward her, stood over her, waited till she sat up. He bent toward her, his face contorted. "I told you," he said. "I told you, I told you," over and over in an unthinking chant. "You bitch. Shut up, shut up!"

Her face was bloodless, the puffed lips pulled back from her teeth, the white teeth looking like bones gleaming from a fracture. She spit at him, clawed at his face with her nails and raked them across his cheek, ripping separate strips of flesh from his face. He slapped her with the back of his hand, brought it forward hard, the heel of his palm thudding into her jaw.

She fell on her back, her skirt sliding up over her knees, baring the white thighs. "You bitch," he said again. "You lousy whore. Well, I touched you. I make you sick, huh? Throw up. Go ahead, vomit, that's what you said, isn't it? I'm not through touching you, damn you."

She stared at him, conscious but stunned, her hands beneath her pressing against the floor. He reached to the neckline of her dress, grabbed the cloth and jerked it, ripping it down the front. With both hands he seized the dress and tore it from her body, ripped the white slip and pulled it from her, threw it across the room.

She stared at him, swore filthily into his face, called him the lowest names she could think of, and her hate and icy contempt fed his fury. He grabbed her arm and wound one hand in her hair, pulled her over the carpet into the bedroom, then picked her up and threw her onto the bed. He stared at her sprawled half across the bed feeling a perverse, dark passion rising in him, swelling hotly in his stomach and loins.

He wound his strong fingers in the brassiere and ripped it from her body, seeing the red marks he left on her white skin. She hissed at him, swore, lips splitting and blood trickling onto her chin. "Get away from me! You filthy, rotten—don't touch me. You beast, you filthy, crazy—"

He hit her with his fist, knocked her back across the bed, then grabbed the pink step-ins and shredded them in his hands, ripped them free of her hips and dropped them to the floor. She moaned, stirred on the bed, only barely conscious.

"You whore," he swore at her, rage leaping like fire in his brain, searing him, piling fuel on the dark and evil hunger surging in him as he stared at her. He swore at her as she moved, shook her head. He pulled the clothes from his body, threw them onto the bed beside her, then crouched naked over her. Her eyes were open, staring at him.

"Tony, don't," she said, the words squeezed separately from her bleeding lips. "Don't."

He held her as she struggled, pitifully weak in the grip of his muscled arms. He pressed himself against her, pinned her wrists with his hands, used his greater strength to force himself upon her, twisting her limbs with ridiculous ease, the fire surging and leaping inside him, the hunger swirling in his loins until the hunger was fed.

When he released her and stood beside the bed, she pulled the spread quickly over her nakedness. Tony looked down at her bruised and battered face, calmness coming over him, and shame beginning to make itself felt. His own nakedness seemed to add to the growing shame and he quickly dressed. Maria's dark eyes stared at him, never leaving his face for a second. Neither spoke until Tony was dressed.

The rage and shame mingled in him, fluttered in his stomach and mind. He pulled wadded bills from his pocket, peeled a ten-dollar bill from his roll, crumpled it in his fist and threw it on the bed.

"There, you bitch. That's just about what you were always worth. Find yourself another sucker; you've still got your moneymaker."

She didn't speak, kept looking directly at his face, staring at him strangely. Something wasn't right; the thought nibbled at his brain. He'd missed something. Something was—the gun. The automatic had been in his coat pocket. It wasn't there now. He felt for it again, looked at Maria.

She was smiling at him, smiling horribly with her face twisted and puffed and bleeding, looking ugly, with the dark eyes wide and staring. Something moved beneath the bedspread she had so quickly thrown over her body, and suddenly Tony knew she held the gun there in one small hand, pointing the lethal bore at him.

He stared at the spot beneath the spread so close to him, saw it move slightly.

"Maria," he said. "Wait." His voice was soft, hardly a whisper in his tightened throat.

She stared into his eyes, almost as if she were not looking at him but at something slimy and revolting. Her face twitched slightly.

He said, "Maria, sweetheart—"

And then the world exploded in his face, the roar of the automatic filled his ears and a massive weight was hurled into his chest. He felt himself thrown backwards, falling, the walls and ceiling and lights spinning crazily as the roaring continued and mounted in his ears. There was a great numbness all through him; he tried to comprehend what it was that had happened to him, but his brain was frozen in a growing panic and his vision blurred.

There was a grayness all around him, a heaviness and stinging in his chest. He could feel a cold chill upon him and knew that he was dying. For a moment the grayness brightened and he felt arms about his head and fingers on his cheeks. Then, close to his face, looming terribly in his eyes, was the bruised and beaten flesh that was almost the face of his Maria. But it was twisted and queerly out of shape, unlike Maria's face, with ugly puffing lips and great staring eyes.

The great eyes moved downward toward him, the ugly lips moved and twisted, parted close to his mouth.

He tried to crawl from that as panic shuddered in him. He tried to shrink away. And he could not.

THE
END

**Don't Let the Mystery End Here.
Try These Other Great Books From
HARD CASE CRIME!**

The Colorado Kid
by STEPHEN KING
WORLD'S BEST-SELLING NOVELIST

When a dead body turns up on a beach off the coast of Maine,
two veteran newspaper reporters begin an investigation that
remains unsolved after 25 years…

Say It With Bullets
by RICHARD POWELL
AUTHOR OF 'A SHOT IN THE DARK'

Bill Wayne's bus tour through the West becomes more than he
bargained for when bodies start turning up at every stop!

The Last Match
by DAVID DODGE
AUTHOR OF 'TO CATCH A THIEF'

From the casinos of Monaco to the jungles of Brazil, from
Tangier to Marrakech to Peru, the chase is on when a handsome
swindler tries to escape the beautiful heiress out to reform him.

**To order, visit www.HardCaseCrime.com or call
1-800-481-9191 (10am to 9pm EST).**
Each title just $6.99 ($8.99 in Canada), plus shipping and handling.

More Fine Books From
HARD CASE CRIME!

The Gutter and the Grave
by ED McBAIN
MWA GRANDMASTER

Detective Matt Cordell was happily married once, and gainfully employed, and sober. But that was before he caught his wife cheating on him with one of his operatives.

The Guns of Heaven
by PETE HAMILL
ACCLAIMED JOURNALIST

Terrorists from Northern Ireland plan to strike in New York City—and only one newspaper reporter stands in their way.

Night Walker
by DONALD HAMILTON
CREATOR OF 'MATT HELM'

When Navy lieutenant David Young came to in a hospital bed, his face was covered with bandages and the nurses were calling him by a stranger's name...

To order, visit www.HardCaseCrime.com or call
1-800-481-9191 (10am to 9pm EST).
Each title just $6.99 ($8.99 in Canada), plus shipping and handling.

Get The Complete First Year of

HARD CASE CRIME

...and Save More Than 30%!

If you missed any of the books from Hard Case Crime's debut year, this is your chance to get them all—at a savings of more than 30% off the cover price! Twelve great books including three Edgar Award nominees, two Shamus Award nominees, and oustanding crime classics by some of the most popular mystery writers of all time:

GRIFTER'S GAME by *Lawrence Block*
FADE TO BLONDE by *Max Phillips*
TOP OF THE HEAP by *Erle Stanley Gardner*
LITTLE GIRL LOST by *Richard Aleas*
TWO FOR THE MONEY by *Max Allan Collins*
THE CONFESSION by *Domenic Stansberry*
HOME IS THE SAILOR by *Day Keene*
KISS HER GOODBYE by *Allan Guthrie*
361 by *Donald E. Westlake*
PLUNDER OF THE SUN by *David Dodge*
BRANDED WOMAN by *Wade Miller*
DUTCH UNCLE by *Peter Pavia*

Find out why critics have called Hard Case Crime "the best new American publisher to appear in the last decade" and why *Entertainment Weekly*, *USA Today*, *The New York Times*, and the *Sunday Morning* program on CBS have all run raves about our books. All for less than $5 per book (plus just 25 cents per book for shipping)!

To order, call 1-800-481-9191
(10am to 9pm EST) and ask for the
Complete First Year of Hard Case Crime.

All 12 books for just $58 (plus $3 for shipping; US orders only)